Lit Crit Guides

# Reading and Interpreting the Works of

# MAYA ANGELOU

Enslow Publishing
101 W. 23rd Street
Suite 240
New York, NY 10011
USA
enslow.com

Audrey Borus

Published in 2018 by Enslow Publishing, LLC
101 W. 23rd Street, Suite 240, New York, NY 10011



**Cataloging-in-Publication Data**
Names: Borus, Audrey.
Title: Reading and interpreting the works of Maya Angelou / Audrey Borus.
Description: New York : Enslow Publishing, 2018 | Series: Lit crit guides | Includes bibliographic references and index. | Audience: Grades 7-12.
Identifiers: ISBN 9780766084971 (library bound)
Subjects: LCSH: Angelou, Maya--Juvenile literature. | African American women authors--Biography--Juvenile literature. | Authors, American--20th century?Biography--Juvenile literature.
Classification: LCC PS3551.N464 Z678 2018 | DDC 818/.5409--dc23

Printed in China

10 9 8 7 6 5 4 3 2 1

**To Our Readers:** We have done our best to make sure all website addresses in this book were active and appropriate when we went to press. However, the author and the publisher have no control over and assume no liability for the material available on those websites or on any websites they may link to. Any comments or suggestions can be sent by e-mail to customerservice@enslow.com.

**Photo Credits:** Cover, p. 1 Ken Charnock/Getty Images; p. 4 Deborah Feingold/Corbis/Getty Images; pp. 7, 69 Buyenlarge/Archive Photos/Getty Images; p. 11 Underwood Archives/Archive Photos/Getty Images; p. 16 Everett Collection; p. 21 Don Cravens/The LIFE Images Collection/Getty Images; pp. 25, 43, 60, 76 Bettmann/Getty Images; p. 30 New York Post Archives/Getty Images; p. 36 Kristoffer Tripplaar/Alamy Stock Photo; p. 40 Library of Congress/Corbis Historical/Getty Images; p. 47 Smith Collection/Gado/Archive Photos/Getty Images; p. 49 Keystone-France/Gamma-Keystone/Getty Images; p. 51 CBS Photo Archive/Getty Images; p. 65 Loomis Dean/The LIFE Picture Collection/Getty Images; p. 79 Moses Robinson/WireImage/Getty Images; p. 85 Michael Ochs Archives/Getty Images; p. 89 © AP Images; p. 95 Jeff Schear/Getty Images; p. 98 Fotos International/Archive Photos/Getty Images; p. 100 Brian Ach/WireImage/Getty Images; p. 102 John D. Kisch/Separate Cinema Archive/Moviepix/Getty Images; p. 104 John Gress/Corbis Entertainment/Getty Images; p. 106 Walter McBride/Corbis Entertainment/Getty Images.

# Contents

Maya Angelou

# 1
# "Strong Black Birds of Promise"

Much has been written by and about Maya Angelou, from screenplays to poetry, memoirs to cookbooks. In her lifetime, Angelou held jobs as a short-order cook, a nightclub entertainer, and a professor of American studies at Wake Forest University. But who was Maya Angelou? What about her and her writing prompted biographer (and close friend) Dolly McPherson to claim "I know of no other autobiographer in American letters who celebrates and sings her life with as much verve and vulnerability as Maya Angelou."[1]

She was born Marguerite Johnson on April 4, 1928, in St. Louis, Missouri, to Bailey and Vivian Baxter Johnson. Marguerite's older brother, Bailey Jr., was her idol and playmate. It was Bailey who provided the first part of Angelou's pen name: As a toddler he called her Maya for "my sister."[2]

## Early Years

When Marguerite was three and Bailey four, their parents divorced and the children were shipped off to Stamps, Arkansas, to their paternal grandmother, Annie Henderson. Henderson (who Bailey and Maya called "Momma") owned the William Johnson General Merchandise Store with her son Willie. The family was able to survive the economic depression of the 1930s because they sold basic staples like beans and flour and made wise investments. Sister Henderson lent money to blacks and whites and used her economic wisdom as clout when anyone was in arrears. She was truly the children's first role model. Confident, strong, and strict, she taught them the virtues of cleanliness, godliness, and respect.

Stamps, Arkansas, was a far cry from Long Beach, California, where the family been living together. It was small, segregated, and racist. There was a long history of mistrust between whites and blacks. Most African Americans in Stamps were poor and worked picking cotton. Life as a cotton picker was hard: the workers put in long hours at the backbreaking labor, and the cotton bolls were so sharp they could tear off skin. Maya and her brother watched as neighbors came into their grandmother's store every morning, hopeful that they would earn enough to pay their bills. And most every night they would return tired, discouraged, and aching. Angelou's biographers have suggested that it was the early experience in

## Long Beach, California in the 1920s

Only twenty-two miles (thirty-five kilometers) from Los Angeles, the port city of Long Beach was originally an Indian trading post. In the late 1800s, it was settled and promoted as a beach resort and, because of its 8.5-mile (13.6-km) beachfront, dubbed "Long Beach." By 1910, the US film industry, which had its start in New York, moved to California in large part because of its famously hospitable climate (which meant less money and time wasted waiting for good weather). "More than an industry, moviemaking cemented California in the national consciousness as a land of sun and dreams. The industry brought more than just wealth; by the 1920s, the mere presence of actor-celebrities attracted visitors from across the nation, while others moved to the city seeking their own fame."[3] It was to this promised land that Angelou's father migrated.

Stamps that shaped Angelou's writing: "The many aphorisms and maxims that particularly find expression in Angelou's earliest works were learned in Stamps, as was her old-fashioned courtesy."[4] The experience also informed the children of what it was like to live with segregation: They "watched and learned about African Americans' grave oppression."[5]

In addition to Momma, Maya and Bailey were supervised by their uncle Willie. Willie had been paralyzed on his right side, allegedly by a fall suffered when someone other than his mother had been minding him. He did not work in the cotton fields, but he did help in the store and he made sure the Johnson children were well-educated. He was "strict and careful about their accuracy and accountability"[6] and more than once threatened to throw them in the store's red-hot potbellied stove if

**aphorism**

A statement of truth; an adage.

**maxim**

A commonly held truth.

In the 1930s there were still cotton pickers in rural Arkansas.

they failed to do their work correctly. Fortunately Maya and Bailey were apt pupils and learned quickly. The children were expected to perform household chores as well. They fed the family chickens, mixed ground meal with table scraps for the pigs, and helped in the store.

Throughout Maya and Bailey's childhood, the two were close: confidants, friends, and sounding boards. Though their grandmother and uncle were strict, there was love. Angelou recalled her life then, particularly her time spent in the store, fondly, "Opening the front doors was pulling the ribbon off the unexpected gift."[7] Of her grandmother, she wrote "Her world was bordered on all sides with work, duty, religion and 'her place.' I don't think she ever knew that a deep-brooding love hung over everything she touched."[8]

In 1935, Bailey Sr. came to Stamps to retrieve his children for an extended stay with their mother, who was living in St. Louis. After rural Arkansas, the city took some getting used to. There was a lot more noise, and the buildings were crowded together and soot-covered. Furthermore, as Angelou said, the "Negro section of St. Louis in the mid-thirties had all the finesse of a gold-rush town."[9] It seems Angelou was smitten with her mother, too, despite the fact that while in Stamps she recalled feeling unloved and unwanted. "To describe my mother would be to write about a hurricane in its perfect power. Or the climbing, falling colors of a rainbow."[10] Though trained as a pediatric nurse, Vivian (or Mother Dear, as Bailey Jr took to calling her) earned a living gambling.

When Bailey and Maya first arrived in St. Louis, they lived with their maternal grandparents. The house was bustling with their grandmother Baxter ("a near white woman with police pull"[11] and their three uncles "best known for their unrelenting meanness."[12] After a few months, Maya and Bailey

## St. Louis in the 1930s

In early 1930s St. Louis, as in the rest of the United States, making or selling alcohol was illegal. During the period known as Prohibition, clubs called speakeasies illegally sold alcohol and became gathering places for drinkers, gamblers, and people looking for a good time. Some biographers have suggested that in trying to support her family, Maya's mother was involved in some of this illegal activity in the clubs where she worked.

moved in with their mother and her boyfriend, known as Mr. Freeman. Because her mother was often out, Freeman had the opportunity to make sexual advances toward Maya and raped her. Freeman told her that if she told anyone, he would kill Bailey. Eventually her brother figured out what had happened, and Maya reluctantly revealed the truth. Freeman was tried for his crime but released on a technicality. He was later found dead, probably kicked to death by Angelou's uncles. Subsequently, Maya became mute, believing that her words had the power to kill; not only Freeman, but everyone else: "Just my breath, carrying my words out, might poison people and they'd curl up and die like the black fat slugs that only pretended."[13] When she did speak, it was only to Bailey.

At first, Maya's family was patient with her. But once deemed "healed" by the doctor, they became increasingly frustrated. Maya was punished for "being so uppity,"[14] then beaten by any relative who felt her sullenness and silence were offensive. Suddenly Bailey and Maya found themselves on the train back to Stamps, Arkansas. "I have never known if Momma sent for us, or if the St. Louis family just got fed up with my grim presence."[15] In any case, Bailey was horribly upset and Maya felt responsible for his unhappiness as well.

The simple quiet of Stamps helped Maya to recover, and though her brother was disappointed, he remained supportive. Mrs. Bertha Flowers, a kind woman who was a friend of Momma's (Angelou called her "the aristocrat of Black Stamps"[16]) took a nurturing interest in Maya. They read classics and poetry together. Maya found a passion for reading and memorizing the works of Langston Hughes, W.E.B. Du Bois, and Paul Laurence Dunbar (in fact, the title of her first autobiography, *I Know Why the Caged Bird Sings*, comes from a line in one of his poems. She also read Shakespeare, Charles Dickens, and Edgar Allan Poe. Mrs. Flowers helped Maya understand the importance of words as well as the importance of education. Eventually Maya began to speak again and in 1940 she graduated at the top of her eighth-grade class.

## Adolescence

Shortly after, Momma accompanied Maya to Los Angeles, where Bailey Sr. was now living. Vivian came down from San Francisco to settle them, and when Bailey arrived about one month later, Momma returned to Stamps. Next, Maya, her mother, and brother all moved to Oakland, California, and then finally to San Francisco when her mother remarried.

Maya attended George Washington High School during the day and at night she took drama and dance classes at the California Labor School, a college to which she had won a scholarship. When she was about fifteen, her father invited her to visit him in southern California. She had hoped to make a connection with her father, but the woman he was living with took an instant dislike to Maya and stabbed her. Angelou's father took her to an acquaintance for treatment

Langston Hughes was probably one of the best known figures in the Harlem Renaissance.

and then left her with a friend. Finding herself alone the next morning, Maya made herself food and left. Roaming around the city, she found a junkyard where she chose a car to sleep in. For the next month, she lived in the junkyard with a group of homeless teens who had banded together and supported one another emotionally and financially. After about a month, Maya called her mother and asked to come home.

Maya realized that the experiences in the junkyard had changed her so much that she was "hardly recognizable to myself."[17] Back in San Francisco she struggled with returning to the routine of going to school, and watching her mother and brother fight. She decided to get a job—a decision her mother supported. Seeing an ad for a streetcar conductor, Maya decided that was what she wanted to do. Even though women, especially black women, had never held such a job, Maya returned to the city office day after day until a reluctant secretary gave her the required test. She passed the test and became the first black woman streetcar conductor in San Francisco. Biographer Jacqueline Thursby explains, "Angelou's persistence and success with that job was a foreshadowing of the drive and determination that manifested itself throughout her life."[18]

Maya worked and continued to go to school. She also began to have doubts about her sexuality. She tried talking to her mother, who told her "I made arrangements a long time ago, to have a boy and a girl. Bailey is my boy and you are my girl. The Man upstairs, He don't make mistakes."[19] Unconvinced, Maya began a relationship with a boy in the neighborhood. They had sex, and three weeks later Maya realized she was pregnant. She continued to go to school,

**foreshadowing**

A literary device used to suggest events that may be coming.

and "two days after V-day (August 1945) stood with the San Francisco Summer School class at Mission High School and received [her] diploma."[20] She finally confessed to her mother (who was in Alaska opening a nightclub) that she was going to give birth. Her mother and stepfather were supportive. Maya's son, Clyde Bailey Johnson (nicknamed Guy), was born a few weeks after her high school graduation. She was sixteen.

## Early Adulthood

With a baby and only a high school education, Maya was thrust into adulthood fairly early. Even though her mother was supportive financially and emotionally, Maya wanted to be independent. She took on a number of jobs, one of which was as a cook in a café that specialized in Creole cuisine. Because she took the job without knowing how to cook Creole food, she went to a family friend (Papa Ford) who "had been a grown man when the twentieth century was born."[21] He told her that Creole cooking "[a]in't nothing but onions, green peppers and garlic."[22] So Maya learned on the job. Later, she would teach herself more techniques and publish a cookbook.

Maya's next move was to Los Angeles, where she was a dancer in nightclubs and, for a short time, ran a brothel. But she was afraid of being arrested, so she and her son, Guy, moved back to Stamps. After California, living in the South was unbearable for her; she found it racist and backward. So Maya returned to California and lived with her mother. "The city didn't even know I had been away, and Mother took me and the baby to a room in her new fourteen-room house as if I had just returned from a long intended holiday."[23] Determined to pay her own way, Maya worked as a short-order cook, but the work was oppressive. Maya's mother, ever encouraging, said, "She always knew her 'daughter had great potential' and was determined that if she had anything to do with it, I was going to realize it."[24] Maya hit on the idea of enlisting in the US Army. Though initially accepted, she was eventually turned down because she had attended the California Labor School, thought to be a hotbed for Communists.

With another career avenue closed, Maya moved to Stockton, California, and became part of a dance team called "Poole and Rita." Her partner, R.L. Poole, taught her to master dance routines and introduced her to performing in the spotlight, which she claimed "locked me into a love of performing that continued for many years."[25] When Poole's former dance partner and girlfriend turned up, Maya lost her job.

Maya continued to live in Stockton, finding work as a short-order cook. She fell in love with a married man and worked as a prostitute to support him before she was summoned back to San Francisco. Her mother was ill and had been hospitalized. Her brother, who was by then married, had just lost his wife to tuberculosis and pneumonia. Though grieving, Bailey sensed that Maya had gotten herself into a bad situation in Stockton. He demanded that she retrieve her son (Maya had left him in the care of a babysitter) and move back to San Francisco.

Maya returned, landing a job across the bay in Oakland as the manager of a restaurant. When that job became another dead end, Maya was approached by one of the restaurant's customers, who asked if she would help him sell women's clothing. Though not a "legitimate" business, Maya felt she could make money and take care of Guy. That was not to be. The clothing supplier had a heroin habit and showed Maya the horror of the drug by injecting himself in front of her, an act Maya interpreted as one of extreme kindness. "I had walked the precipice and seen it all; and at the critical moment, one man's generosity pushed me safely away from the edge."[26] The episode was enough to make her return to San Francisco and search for more mainstream work.

## Marriage and the Stage

When her son, Guy, was about five, Maya began working at a record store in the Fillmore district, a part of San Francisco known as "the Harlem of the West." One of the store's regular customers, Enistasious "Tosh" Angelos, became interested in Maya. A Greek American, Angelos had served in the US Navy and was working in San Francisco. Against her mother's wishes, Maya married him in 1949 and became the prototypical 1950s housewife: she cooked, cleaned, and dedicated herself to her husband and son. Guy, for his part, became attached to Angelos. So it was particularly difficult for him when three years later, the marriage dissolved.

One remnant of the failed union was Maya's surname: Using the feminine version of Tosh's name ("Angelou") she officially became Maya Angelou and fabricated a new background for herself. She told people she was Cuban-African in order to become a calypso dancer at the famous San Francisco nightclub the Purple Onion. From there, she was noticed as an exceptional dancer and singer and was invited to act in a State Department production of the play *Porgy and Bess.* With the State Department acting company, Angelou toured twenty-two countries, spanning Europe, the Middle East, and Russia. While in Paris, France, she met and established a friendship with the writer James Baldwin.

## Move to New York

By now in her late twenties, Angelou realized that by moving around so much she was giving her son the same kind of childhood she had experienced. So she vowed to either take work in the Bay Area or take Guy with her. Angelou was writing short pieces and music lyrics and recorded several of her songs for a record called *Miss Calypso*. While recording she met the author John Killens, who was working on a screenplay of his novel *Youngblood*. Killens suggested that Angelou move to New York and join the Harlem Writers Guild. From them, he

Maya Angelou had many talents and held many jobs over the years. Here she is as a calypso dancer in 1957.

## Porgy and Bess

The opera *Porgy and Bess* began its life as a novel called *Porgy*. Written by white South Carolinian Dubose Heyward in 1925, the work was adapted into a play by his wife, Dorothy, and, in 1935, a "folk" opera with music written by George Gershwin and libretto (lyrics) by Heyward.

The storyline is pretty typical for opera: Boy meets girl, boy loses girl, boy gets her back. Set in 1920s Charleston, South Carolina, in a black neighborhood called Catfish Row, the play tells the story of Porgy, a lame beggar who uses a goat-drawn cart to get around. He falls in love with Bess, a woman of uncertain reputation who is under the thumb of a thug named Crown. When Crown kills a Catfish Row inhabitant in a crap game, he must leave. When Crown returns for Bess, Porgy kills him. Porgy goes to jail, and Bess hooks up with another flashy gambler called Sportin' Life. At the close of the story, Porgy is out of jail and heading to New York to search for Bess.

What was unusual about the opera was the fact that its cast was all black. There was criticism and controversy, including accusations of racial stereotyping. John von Rhein, a critic for the *Chicago Tribune*, described the play as "a tale about disadvantaged Southern blacks by a white novelist, DuBose Heyward, set to music by a Jewish songwriter-lyricist team from New York"[27] but went on to say that the play "did not flinch from confronting issues of race and class. Those issues—grinding poverty, domestic abuse, racist bigotry, crime, drugs and prostitution—remain very much with us today."[28]

assured her, she would receive honest and useful criticism that would improve her writing. Angelou decided to follow Killen's advice and she and Guy moved to New York City. It was 1959. Guy was fourteen and Angelou thirty-one.

The Harlem Writers Guild was not just concerned with writing. The members were involved in a host of contemporary issues—civil rights and African independence among them. Thus, Angelou's writing became more informed politically. At the same time, other members' criticisms made her realize that good writing was hard work (documented in *The Heart of Woman*).

As Angelou's involvement with the Harlem Writers Guild continued, her interest in civil rights grew. Though initially uncomfortable with talk of racial oppression, Angelou joined Martin Luther King Jr., Ralph Abernathy, and others to challenge segregation. She and actor/comedian Godfrey Cambridge met and organized a fund-raiser for King's Southern Christian Leadership Conference (SCLC), a group of young ministers who believed that the church had a responsibility to act in the political arena. The SCLC was their vehicle for coordinating activism. The fund-raiser took the form of a cabaret which ran for five weeks at the Village Vanguard, a famous nightclub in Greenwich Village, New York City. When it was over, Angelou became coordinator of the SCLC's New York office.

In the early 1960s, John Killens introduced Angelou to African activist Vusumi Make. Make was in New York speaking to the United Nations about South African apartheid (a legal system of racist oppression which was practiced in that country). She had been hearing about his speech from her friends and coworkers and had drawn a mental picture of him: tall and older than she. But when she actually met him, she

## Black Artists and the Harlem Writers Guild

The Harlem Writers Guild (or "Club," as it was originally called) was started in the 1950s by a core group of African American writers who felt that their work was being excluded from the mainstream press. Some of the members had been to prestigious universities and had tried to break into the white world of publishing. But they found it unrewarding and maintained that white critics and writers could not fully appreciate black American literature.

John Oliver Killens, Rosa Guy, and John Henrik Oliver were among the founding members who were looking for an alternative place to hone their craft. Killens, who had studied at Columbia and New York University, invited other writers to join him at a Harlem storefront on the corner of 125th Street and Lenox Avenue to critique each other's work. This was in 1950. As members of the group became published, they decided to change their name from "Harlem Writers Club" to "Harlem Writers Guild" to emphasize that writing was craft.

Among the seminal works published were Killens's 1954 book *Youngblood*, the story of a family and its struggles against racism in Georgia; Rosa Guy's *Bird at My Window* (1966), an account of Guy's struggles growing up in Harlem; and the play *Ceremonies in Dark Old Men* by Lonne Elder III, whose work was produced by the newly-formed Negro Ensemble Company in 1969 and later adapted for television.

By 1983, founder Killens estimated that guild members had published more than four hundred literary works. Actors like Sidney Poitier, Amiri Baraka, Ossie Davis, and Harry Belafonte began to join the guild as well. Angelou met them all when she joined.

was surprised. In *The Heart of a Woman*, she recalls, "He was three inches shorter than I and his baby face was surrounded by fat."[29] By the end of the next evening, they become involved, and though Angelou was engaged to another man at the time, the two end up moving in together.

About 1961, Angelou was offered a part in *The Blacks*, a play written by French author Jean Genet. Initially, she was reluctant. "*The Blacks* was a white foreigner's idea of a people he did not understand. Genet had superimposed the meanness and cruelty of his own people onto a race he had never known, a race already nearly doubled over carrying the white man's burden of greed and guilt, and which at the same time toted its own insufficiency."[30] Her partner Make didn't want her to take it either, claiming, "No wife of an African leader can go on stage."[31] This irked Angelou, but she said nothing. In fact, since their initial union, Angelou had begun to notice Make's chauvinism: his insistence that she keep the house just so, his disapproval of her choices in furniture and wallpaper. Still, Angelou felt that he was a necessary father figure for Guy.

Finally, after speaking to one of Angelou's friends, Make read the play and decided she must perform. Angelou took the part of the White Queen, a character she used to "ridicule mean white women and brutal white men who had too often injured me and mine."[32] The play was well received. But Angelou began getting threatening calls at the theater. The calls informed her that Make was at risk. When she told Make, he explained that these tactics were a common ploy of the South African police: "They do that sort of thing. Telephone the wives of freedom fighters and tell them their husbands or their children have been killed…I guess I should be insulted that they are just beginning on you."[33] The calls continued; one even sent Angelou to the hospital in search of her son who

Angelou knew and was inspired by the famous civil rights leader Martin Luther King Jr.

had allegedly been knifed. After that incident, she decided not to cave in to any doubts she had about Make—she would try and make their relationship work.

Though *The Blacks* had been successful, Angelou's interactions with the play's producer, a white man, were not. After the show's musical director had quit, Angelou had stepped forward to work on music. When she asked to be paid for that work, the producer would not hear of it. Angelou attributed this to his being an "arrogant thie[f] who took the work of black artists."[34] With Make's help, she broke her contract and left the show. At this time, she also discovered that Make had not been paying the bills. They were evicted from their apartment and Make moved them to Cairo, Egypt.

## Heart of a Woman

Angelou and her son were captivated by Egypt. Make had gone ahead and found an elegant apartment, and Guy was enrolled in an American private high school where he did exceedingly well. But money was still a problem, as Angelou learned from the maid she had hired. All the lush furniture and rugs had been rented and payment had not been made. Furthermore, Guy's school began to send notices of missed payments. Angelou was again in the position of being dependent on Make, while his chauvinism made it impossible for her to even broach the topic of work. In Cairo, with the help of an American journalist, Angelou got a job as associate editor for a newspaper. Initially, Make would not allow it, but after Angelou convinced him that her working would allow him to contribute more money to freedom fighters in South Africa, he relented.

From 1960 to 1961, Angelou worked at the *Arab Observer*. At about this time, Angelou realized she was no longer in love.

In addition to being financially irresponsible, Make became involved with other women. Once Guy finished high school, Angelou left Egypt and Make and traveled with her son to Accra, Ghana, where he was to attend the University of Ghana. Angelou secured a job in Liberia. But her plans changed when Guy was involved in a car accident. His arm, leg, and neck were broken. He recovered after several months, and Angelou was able to pull strings so that he could attend the university. Once he had recovered, Angelou allowed herself to really appreciate Ghana: "Accra became a wondrous city as Guy's health improved. The sprawling Makola market drew me into its heaving perfumed bosom, and held me there for hours."[35] Rather than go on to Liberia, Angelou decided to stay in Accra.

Settling in Ghana was not insignificant. Writes critic Dolly McPherson, "Unlike Liberia, which was founded by former American Slaves, Ghana is culturally African…The attraction to Ghana is both symbolic and cultural for, like many Blacks, Angelou perceives it to be a lost home,"[36] a fact made clear when flying over the African continent, she noted, "I could look down from my window seat and see trees, and bushes, rivers and dense forest. It all began here."[37]

## God's Children

Though she lived very economically, Angelou needed money. With the help of friends, she landed a job as an administrator at the School of Music and Drama at the University of Ghana. "Guy was seventeen and quick. I was thirty-three and determined. We were Black Americans in West Africa, where for the first time in our lives the color of our skin was accepted as correct and normal."[38]

Next, Angelou was hired to work for the *Ghanaian Times*. She learned to speak Fanti so as to "get behind the face of modern Ghana [and] get a glimpse of Africa's ancient tribal soul."[39] She got her hair "fixed Ghanaian fashion" and joined the National Council of Ghana Women. She acquired a whole range of women friends: academics, artists, and expatriates. But even as Angelou's love affair with Ghana grew, she experienced some of the same self-doubt she had in the United States. When she was offered part-time work with the Ghanaian Broadcasting service and turned up at their offices, a black receptionist treated her poorly. Angelou fought back with her tongue—despite the fact that the receptionist and she "could have been sisters, or in fact, might be cousins far removed."[40] Angelou responded "as if she was a rude White salesclerk in an American department store."[41] But the incident was sobering. It forced Angelou to examine herself: "Was it possible that I and all American Blacks had been wrong on other occasions? Could the cutting treatment we often experienced have been stimulated by something than our features, our hair and color? Was the odor of old slavery so obvious that people were offended and lashed out at us automatically?"[42]

Meanwhile, back in the United States, the civil rights movement was gaining more momentum. The March on Washington was being planned, but the group of people with whom Angelou was now friendly were much more radical than those people she had known and respected during her days as an organizer for Dr. King. "We were brave revolutionaries, not pussyfooting nonviolent cowards. We scorned the idea of being spat upon, kicked and then turning our cheeks for more abuse."[43] Angelou kept quiet about her work for King, but someone suggested that as black Americans, the expatriates should support the march and picket the United States Embassy in Accra. So along with others in the expatriate community, Angelou organized a parallel march.

Maya Angelou made the acquaintance of many influential black leaders, including Malcolm X, a black nationalist and Muslim leader in the 1950s and early 1960s.

Malcolm X arrived in Accra. Angelou had met him in New York when he was "the bombastic spokesman for Elijah Muhammad's Nation of Islam."[44] The Nation of Islam regarded all white people as "blue-eyed devils." Malcolm X had been particularly condemning in his beliefs about whites. However, having toured Africa, he had come to the conclusion that not all whites *were* devils, "nor that any human being was inherently cruel at birth,"[45] and he broke with the Nation of Islam. Angelou used her influence and connections to get Malcolm an audience with the Ghanaian president, Kwame Nkrumah. After that meeting Angelou accompanied him to the airport. On the way there, Malcolm told Angelou she needed to grow up in her fight against racism. "Don't be in such a hurry to condemn a person because he doesn't do what you do or think as you think or as fast," he told her.[46] "When you hear that the Urban League or the NAACP is giving a formal banquet at the Waldorf-Astoria, I know you won't go, but don't knock them. They give scholarships to poor Black children. One of those recipients might become a Julian Mayfield, or a Maya Angelou, or a Malcolm X."[47]

The year was 1964 and Guy, then nineteen, informed his mother it was time for him to have his own life. At first, Angelou did not want to accept this: "His existence had defined my own. As a child his sense of humor, attraction for puns and affection for me had lightened the single parent burden."[48] But Angelou realized that she needed to let him separate, and to do so she had to leave Ghana.

Miraculously, an opportunity presented itself. Theaters in Berlin and Venice wanted to stage a revival of the Genet play *The Blacks* with the original cast. Angelou jumped at the chance to work with her old cast members. As Angelou flew to Germany, she observed that simply hearing the

German language evoked memories of seeing photographs of Auschwitz survivors and reading John Hersey's *The Wall*. "In Ghana I worked hard at forgiving those African chiefs who collaborated in the slave trade, but couldn't find it in my heart to exonerate the stewardesses who were toddlers at the time of the Holocaust. Prejudice is a burden which confuses the past, threatens the future, and renders the present inaccessible."[49]

Upon her return to Ghana, Angelou received correspondence from Malcolm X describing his work to build the Organization for Afro-American Unity (OAAU). In 1965, Angelou decided she could leave her near-grown son and return to the United States to help build Malcolm's organization.

## Flung Up to Heaven

Angelou flew into New York with the intention of starting with Malcolm right away. However, when she arrived she realized that after living out of the country for four years, she needed to reacclimate. She flew on to San Francisco, where her mother and brother were waiting. Though supportive as always, Angelou's mother did not approve of her alliance with Malcolm X: "I read in the papers that you were coming back to work with Malcolm X in some new organization. I really hope not…If you feel you have to do that—work for no money—go back to Martin Luther King. He's really trying to help our people. Malcolm X is a rabble-rouser."[50] Less than forty-eight hours later, Malcolm X was dead, assassinated by three members of the Nation of Islam.

Angelou felt Malcolm's loss intensely. With nothing on the horizon, she traveled with her brother to Hawaii, where he was then living and working as a chef. Bailey Jr. convinced her to resume dancing and singing, which she did for six months before realizing that what she wanted to do was write. But she had no desire to be in New York. Instead she went to Los Angeles, where she worked part-time as a market researcher and used the rest of her waking hours to write.

The market research work involved asking housewives about the kind of products they used. Angelou was assigned to Watts, an area that she had once been familiar with. "I was disappointed to find it had lost its air of studied grace. I had known the area when it had a kind of staid decorum, a sort of church-ladies-display-at-a-Sunday-afternoon tea feeling."[51] When riots erupted in the summer of 1965, Angelou was not surprised. She knew many of the residents were unemployed, lacked education, and were part of street gangs. She attributed some of the unrest to the fact that families had fallen apart. "Dinners together became fewer because the father was seldom there and the mother was busy reviewing where she went wrong…The bootless children, with discipline removed, without the steadying hand of a present parent who cared began to run like young tigers in the streets…Gangs of abandoned children bullied their way up and down the sidewalks of Watts, growing bolder and angrier every day."[52]

Rosa Guy, Angelou's friend from the Harlem Writers Guild, was visiting Los Angeles to promote one of her books. She convinced Angelou to return to New York and write seriously again. Angelou was all set to go, but Guy (who had returned to the United States) was hit by a truck in San Francisco. Once again, his neck was broken but his prognosis was for a full recovery.

Angelou finally moved back to New York, where she resumed her friendship with writer James Baldwin. He introduced her to his family, who welcomed her and considered her a blood relation. However, when Baldwin decided to move to California to support the Black Panther Party, he and Angelou had a falling out. Despite her having supported Malcolm X, Angelou was again in favor of Dr. King's passive resistance movement. The declared violence of the Black Panthers did not appeal to Angelou as a way to encourage real change in race relations. Though she approved of the Panthers in general, she though Eldridge Cleaver, one of their leaders, was "an opportunist and a batterer."[53] Baldwin argued, "You can't separate Cleaver from the Panthers. He is their general."[54] Eventually, Angelou and Baldwin were able to see beyond their differences.

In 1968, Dr. King asked Angelou to help raise funds for another Washington march. Pleased to be asked, Angelou was ready to begin work. But on April 4 (Angelou's birthday), she learned that King had been assassinated. Crushed, she turned to Baldwin, who helped her channel her grief into serious writing. Angelou also began working on a ten-part television series called *Black, Blues, Black*. She wrote the show's transcript, hosted it, and performed in it as well.

Through James Baldwin, Angelou had met the cartoonist Jules Feiffer and his wife Judy, with whom she enjoyed socializing and telling stories about her experiences. Around this time, the couple contacted an editor at Random House named Robert Loomis. They told Loomis about Angelou and Loomis contacted her, suggesting that she write an autobiography. Though she demurred, Loomis continued to be in touch. Then he got a tip from Baldwin about how to win Angelou over: present her with a challenge. So Loomis called Angelou and mentioned that autobiography was one of the hardest genres to write well. Taking the bait, Angelou agreed to do it. The result was *I Know Why the Caged Bird Sings*. Published in 1970, it was her account of the first sixteen years of her life.

The book was nominated for a National Book Award, became a Book of the Month Club selection, and was also made into a TV movie. Seven more autobiographies followed: *Gather Together in my Name* (1974), *Singin' and Swingin' and Gettin' Merry Like Christmas* (1976), *The Heart of a Woman* (1981), *All God's Children Need Traveling Shoes* (1986), *A Song Flung Up to Heaven* (2002), and *Mom & Me & Mom* (2013).

In 1973, Maya Angelou met and married Paul Du Feu. Du Feu had been married to feminist Germaine Greer and was himself a writer as well as an architect. According to Angelou, Du Feu "taught me to build. He said, 'Building has nothing to do with strength or with sex, or with gender. It has do with insight. If you can see it, you can build it. But you must see it.'"[55] The couple remained together for nearly ten years before they divorced in 1981. Angelou chronicled some of those years in her collection of essays called *Even the Stars Look Lonesome* (1997). That same year, she published her fourth autobiography (*The Heart of a Woman*) and was appointed Reynolds Professor and Chair

Paul du Feu was Angelou's second husband. The couple met and married in 1973.

of American Studies at Wake Forest University in Winston-Salem, North Carolina.

For the next twelve years, Angelou taught at Wake Forest and continued to write and perform. In 1983, she published a collection of poetry called *Shaker, Why Don't You Sing* and in 1986, she published her next autobiography, *All God's Children Need Traveling Shoes*. That same year, she traveled to Liberia as a guest lecturer and also appeared in a PBS documentary with host Bill Moyers. Though the two had grown up in the South no more than 30 miles (48 km) apart, their worlds could not have been more different. In 1988, the two teamed up again to film *Facing Evil*, the proceedings of a conference in central Texas on the theme of evil, a topic about which Angelou thought a lot. Angelou told those gathered:

> We need the courage to create ourselves daily, to be bodacious enough to create ourselves daily—as Christians, as Jews, as Muslims, as thinking, caring, laughing, loving human beings. I think that the courage to confront evil and turn it by dint of will into something applicable to the development of our evolution, individually and collectively, is exciting, honorable.[56]

She also traveled to London to direct a revival of a play by Trinidadian playwright Errol John called *Moon over a Rainbow Shawl*.

In 1990, Angelou published another poetry collection called *I Shall Not Be Moved*. She dedicated it to her mother, Vivian Baxter. She lectured in Washington, DC, and began appearing regularly in mainstream media. But 1993 came her biggest and perhaps most visible honor: She was asked to write and read a poem for the inauguration of President Bill

Clinton. Angelou was the first poet to read at an inauguration since Robert Frost read at John F. Kennedy's ceremony in 1961.

"On the Pulse of Morning" is over one hundred lines and was televised around the world. Critic Mary Jane Lupton noted, "The poem, like the incoming president offered the dream of hope—for Native Americans, gays, homeless, Eskimos, Jews, West Africans, Muslims."[57] It wasn't just the poem itself, but Angelou's delivery of it—what one biographer called "theatrical but always reverent"[58] that made an impression on many listeners.

Critics have suggested that since Angelou wrote so extensively about herself, many people feel they know her well and "treat [her] as public property."[59] It may also be because of the fact that Angelou's delivery was a mixture of down-home

## Million Man March

On October 16, 1995, Louis Farrakhan, leader of the Nation of Islam, organized a mass gathering of black men in Washington, DC. It was called the Million Man March. Reminiscent of the civil rights marches three decades before, the purpose of the march was to counter the negative stereotype of the black American male. That same day, another event, Day of Absence, was organized by black female leaders. This event was meant to encourage those who could not attend the gathering in Washington to participate in local events emphasizing positive engagement in black communities around the United States. The exact number of participants in Washington, DC, was not determined, but estimates ranged from four hundred thousand to two million people in attendance. Angelou was one of the speakers and she wrote and read her "Million Man March" poem for the occasion.

Southern politeness, aphorisms, and charm. British journalist Gary Younge wrote that seeing her on stage was like "watching stand-up comedy, a university lecture and a poetry recital all in one. With stories, quips and poems—both her own and those of African-American poets both dead and living—she has them laughing, gasping and listening for over an hour."[60]

In 1994, one year after her presidential performance, Random House published *The Collected Poems of Maya Angelou* and teamed up with photographer Margaret Courtney-Clarke to publish a children's book called *My Painted House, My Friendly Chicken, and Me.* In 1995, Bantam Books recognized Angelou for being the first black American to have the longest running nonfiction title on the *New York Times* bestseller list. That same year, Angelou read her poem "A Brave and Startling Truth" at the United Nations fiftieth anniversary party. In October she also recited a poem that she wrote for the Million Man March.

Angelou became an ambassador for the United Nations Children's Fund in 1996. She also published a second children's book called *Koji and his Magi*c and appeared in a popular network TV series called *Touched by an Angel.* During the late 1990s, she published essays, appeared on *The Oprah Winfrey Show* (she and Winfrey were close friends), directed a screenplay called *Down in the Delta*, and continued to win numerous awards, including *Writer's Digest's* 100 Best Writers of the 20th Century award.

In 2000, Angelou signed on with Hallmark Cards to launch the Maya Angelou Collection from Hallmark. Critics were harsh: poet laureate Billy Collins was quoted as saying, "I think it's preposterous, it lowers the understanding of what poets can do"[61] and "I thought that it was odd that a poet of her stature would sign a contract with Hallmark, seeing that

'Hallmark' has always been synonymous with sentimental verse."[62] Even the TV program *Saturday Night Live* lampooned her. But Angelou thought it was the perfect medium to spread her message: "What's wrong," she asked, "with wanting 'to put poetry in people's hands, even if they're not going to buy a book?' She quotes Nathaniel Hawthorne: 'Easy reading is the hardest writing.'"[63]

Angelou continued to write, promote social causes, and teach at Wake Forest. In 2005, she read "Amazing Peace" at the lighting of the National Christmas Tree and also published a collection of poetry with the same name. In 2008, she published *Letter to My Daughter*, in which she proclaimed she was writing for women of all races, shapes, and sizes: "You are Black and White, Jewish and Muslim, Asian, Spanish speaking, Native American and Aleut. You are fat and thin and pretty and plain, gay and straight, educated and unlettered, and I am

## Poetry for the People?

Angelou often said that one of her main goals was to get people to read her work. In an interview with the London *Observer*, she said, "If I'm America's poet, or one of them, I want to be in people's hands. All people's hands, people who would never buy a book."[64] And she dismissed the criticism of those who questioned her choice of creating products for Hallmark as "literary snobbery."[65] Thus, the question is raised: Can good writing be made trivial by its venue? In other words, does the fact that Angelou wrote for Hallmark and was widely consumed by people who were not necessarily readers, make her less authentic or talented? Does her prolific output make her less of a writer or less qualified to write about issues of racism and violence? Or could it be that Angelou made writing looking easy?

speaking to you all."[66] It was the kind of writing that perhaps prompted critic James McWhorter to dub her "Saint Maya."

## The Critics

"Saint Maya" also received her fair share of criticism. Poet Wanda Coleman believed that Angelou's writing was stilted. She wrote a scathing review of one of Angelou's autobiographies (*A Song Flung up to Heaven*), calling it "small and inauthentic, without ideas, wisdom or vision." She ends the review by writing "Something is being flung up to heaven all right, but it isn't a song."[67]

Linguist and social commentator John McWhorter echoes Coleman's sentiments by remarking that "Angelou's writings are the product of a worse and blissfully bygone America. White readers who feel enlightened enough about race issues to have wearied of being lectured about them may be put off by these books today. And a black person likely would not, and really should not, write a memoir in this style today."[68] McWhorter recalls a scene in *The Heart of a Woman* where Angelou describes a summons from the (white) principal at her son's school for his alleged misbehavior. Sitting in that office, Angelou wonders how a white woman could "understand a black mother who had nothing to give her son but contrived arrogance?" McWhorter counters 'contrived arrogance' was once a useful and even natural form of defense against bigotry, but that is no longer true and that Angelou's writing and approach is hopelessly dated.

## Final Years

At a memorial for Michael Jackson in 2009, singer Queen Latifah read "We Had Him," a poem Angelou had written for the occasion. Angelou also wrote an opinion piece for the

In 2010 Angelou received the Presidential Medal of Freedom from President Obama.

*Washington Post*, introducing Michelle Obama to the voting public as Barack Obama began his campaign: "In September 2008, I was invited to introduce Michelle Obama at an event in Greensboro, N.C. I had met her fleetingly during the Democratic National Convention in Boston, but I had no real sense of her personality. I telephoned Oprah Winfrey, aware that she knew the Obamas, and asked, 'What is your take on Michelle Obama?' Oprah answered promptly and with conviction, 'She is the real deal.'"[69] Angelou became friends with Michelle Obama and remained so until her death in 2014, when Mrs. Obama gave the eulogy at a private memorial service.

In 2010, President Barack Obama presented Angelou with the Presidential Medal of Freedom. That same year, Angelou sold her letters and notes to the New York Public Library's Schomburg Center for Research in Black Culture. Included in the collection are letters from James Baldwin, Malcolm X, and Coretta Scott King, as well as many other notable historical figures. Consistent with her belief that her work should be accessible, she told the *New York Times* that at eighty-two it "dawned on her that 'I'd better make sure that my papers and books are taken care of, they are somewhere where people can see them and read them.'"[70]

Well into her eighties, Angelou was "a constant advocate for the continuing civil rights movements and many outreach groups."[71] Her final autobiography, *Mom & Me & Mom*, was published in 2013. Maya Angelou died on May 28, 2014, at her home in Winston-Salem, North Carolina. She was eighty-six years old.

# 2 Defying Odds and Gods—Angelou and Autobiography

In this chapter, we look at autobiography as a literary genre and explore how Angelou conformed to and reshaped ideas about the genre.

Literary scholars have noted that many African American writers have a special connection to autobiography. From the first slave narratives to the present day, "Autobiography is a cornerstone of Afro-American literature,"[1] providing "one of the most powerful forms of black literary expression."[2] Because of their heritage as slaves, black Americans have not always been able to "gain access to truthful explanations of [their] African roots or of [their] historical background in America."[3] So the question, "Who am I?" is particularly poignant in African American writing. Black writers have used autobiography to "share their views, leave a record of their struggles, to inspire future generations and to portray the individual life as the embodiment of larger experience of Black American life."[4]

The word "autobiography" comes from Greek and Latin: *autos* (Greek) meaning "self," *bios* (Greek) meaning "life," and *graphia* (Latin) meaning "story." In other words, the narrative of a person's life. In its purest form, autobiography is written in the first person with the major events of the writer's life recorded in chronological order. Some critics believe that Angelou's prose works are not true autobiography. Rather, they are autobiographical fiction "for the apparent reason that Angelou amplifies the autobiographical tone by using

**first-person narration**

A story that the author tells from his or her point of view.

dialogue—by having another character or characters speak to the narrator."[5] But as professor of English and Angelou biographer Mary Jane Lupton points out, there are plenty of examples of autobiographies that bend the standard definition. One of the most significant is that of James Weldon Johnson, one of Angelou's favorite writers. In his book *The Autobiography of an Ex-Colored Man*, Johnson, a black man, assumes the persona of a white man. He uses characters, locations and incidents from his life, but the voice is not his. Likewise, writer Gertrude Stein wrote *The Autobiography of Alice B. Toklas* from the first person perspective of her partner, Alice Toklas, but was in fact, writing about her own life in the third person.

Though an account of a person's own history, black autobiography is "often a means to present a corrective image of social and political trends and the moral drives and spiritual needs of Black people."[6] Nowhere is this truer than in the autobiographical works of Maya Angelou. While she strives to find an identity and meaning in her own life, Angelou does so in relation to being black and American. By studying her work, we learn not only about her experiences but about American cultural history.

## Serial Autobiography

Typically, an autobiographer tells his or her story in one volume. In a serial autobiography, that story expands over two or more volumes, each volume contributing to a larger picture. Because a serial autobiography is told over time, the author places him or herself in a historical context; that is, he or she become representative of a particular time and place,

James Weldon Johnson was an author, politician, and lawyer. His best known novel, *The Autobiography of an Ex-Colored Man*, may have inspired Angelou's own autobiographical writing.

even if the objective is to write about what makes him or her unique.

The concept is not new. As early as the sixteenth century, the French writer Michel de Montaigne wrote a collection of autobiographical essays. "For years after he first published the *Essays*, Montaigne continued to go back to them, amending them extensively. The resulting text allows scholars to view the process by which his thoughts and opinions evolved over time."[7]

There is a long tradition of black authors who have written serial autobiographies: Paul Laurence Dunbar, Zora Neale Hurston, and Frederick Douglass are just a few. Angelou was adamant about calling her six prose works autobiographies, not novels. For her, autobiography was a conscious choice. In fact, in 1987, she told an interviewer "I think I am the only serious writer who has chosen the autobiographical form as the main form to carry my work, my expression. I pray that in each book I am getting closer to finding the mystery of really manipulating and being manipulated by this medium, to pulling it open, stretching it."[8]

Then there is the playwright Lillian Hellman, who also wrote serial autobiographies. Almost as prolific as Angelou, Hellman wrote four volumes, and the first, *An Unfinished Woman* (1970), won the National Book Award. According to Lupton, it would seem that the women had a lot in common: both had worked in the theater and developed their sense of dialogue there, both wrote about their lives in the United States and abroad, both were publicly praised in their lifetimes.[9] However, Hellman was as well known for her work as for her relationship with the writer Dashiell Hammett. Maya Angelou "had no celebrity status though she had appeared on stage and in clubs: the heart of her memoir writing was, in fact the commonality of her life. Hellman was white; Angelou was not only African American but African American from the Southern United States—and Angelou was largely uneducated in any formal sense. She also wrote, without apology, about the bleak events in the early years of her life—and she did so without blaming mainstream culture—that is, white culture—for those events."[10]

## Telling the Truth

One assumes that an autobiographer does his or her best to represent the truth; at least in so far as they experience it. "Whether or not truth is an ambiguous term and one ultimately ignored either through malice or self-delusion by many autobiographers, it is certain that every autobiographer explicitly or implicitly professes that he will speak the truth—at least about what he has selected to make public."[11] Yet, in an interview, Maya Angelou admitted to "fiddling with" the truth, combining two or more real-life characters into one.[12] This is a conscious choice. Angelou was first and foremost concerned with getting her message to readers. "I want to tell the truth, but I can't because I'd ruin the thing. [Losing] the reader is ruining the thing. If I tell the truth …in language which shocks but does not terrify, which shakes somebody up but doesn't make them run away, I may impart something which might be of help."[13]

Though some have criticized Angelou for taking liberties, others like David Levering Lewis note that Angelou wrote with "such just-rightness of timing and inner truthfulness that each of her books is a continuing autobiography of much of Afro-America. Her ability to shatter the opaque prisms of race and class between reader and subject is her special gift."[14] Biographer Mary Jane Lupton points out, "What frequently

After living in Ghana, Angelou often wore traditional headscarves, despite her initial reaction to them as "a fashion worn by the pickaninnies whose photographs I had seen and hated in old books."

goes unsaid when discussing so-called truth in the history of African American autobiography is that in many instances the truth has been censored or hidden out of the need for self-protection. Black autobiographers writing during the abolitionist movement (the antislavery movement that flourished during the several decades before the Civil War) had to restrain or disguise their opinions, even toward their compassionate editors."[15]

It is interesting to note the changes in tone in Angelou's writing over time. She once said in an interview that "The person I was yesterday is not exactly the same as the person I am today. The person I wrote about 20 years ago knew only that much. Now, writing today, about somebody 20 years ago, one has to impose a kind of distance, otherwise I will imbue that person with the wisdom I have today."[16] Critic Linda Wagner Martin suggests that, compared to four previous works, *All God's Children Need Traveling Shoes* is more "subdued." There are "fewer scenes filled with dialogue, fewer comic episodes, and fewer digressions. It stands as a clear testament to the four years Angelou and Guy spent in Cairo and Ghana, and to the inherent (and highly publicized) relationship between Africa as an essential personal, religious and traditional source."[17] This continues into Angelou's next work, *A Song Flung Up to Heaven* (2002). Reading the books sequentially makes clear the author's consistent honesty, her ability to compress ranges of events so as to give readers clear scenes, complete with natural-sounding dialogue, that illustrate the whole—her excellence in achieving the effects she wants. These qualities also show that Angelou upholds a time-honored African tradition as a memory keeper and a historian.

# 3

# Caged Bird

The first of Angelou's six autobiographies, *I Know Why the Caged Bird Sings* recounts Angelou's tumultuous childhood, her adolescence, and her sudden initiation into adulthood with the birth of her son. It is also a collection of richly drawn, colorful characters: her strict and wise grandmother Annie (Momma) Henderson, her disabled Uncle Willie, her brother Bailey, her dashing father, and her elegant and worldly mother. The book also chronicles Angelou's childhood, especially in the South, and what it was like to be black at a time when civil rights were easily overlooked. "But most of all her story is the story of discovering who she is—working her way through a multifaceted identity crisis."[1] The title of the book comes from a poem called "Sympathy" by Paul Laurence Dunbar. The stanza is as follows:

> *I know why the caged bird sings, ah me,*
> *When his wing is bruised and his bosom sore, —*
> *When he beats his bars and he would be free;*
> *It is not a carol of joy of glee,*
> *But a prayer that he sends from his heart's deep core,*
> *But a plea, that upward to Heaven he flings —*
> *I know why the caged bird sings!*

## Summary

### Part I

Angelou begins *I Know Why the Caged Bird Sings* with a description of herself preparing to recite a poem at church on Easter Sunday. She is wearing a purple taffeta dress she watched her grandmother sew, and she knew that once she put it on, she was going to look like a movie star—a white movie star. In reality, she tells the reader, she is a "too-big Negro girl, with nappy black hair, broad feet and a space between her teeth that would hold a number-two pencil."[2]

In the first chapter, we learn that when Marguerite (Maya) is three and her brother, Bailey, is four, they are sent to live with their paternal grandma (Mrs. Annie Henderson or "Momma" as they call her) in Stamps, Arkansas. Their parents are no longer together. The children's father has pinned their train tickets inside Bailey's coat, tied notes to their wrists stating who they are and where they are going, and then entrusts their care to a railroad porter. (Angelou notes that she later learned this was not an uncommon practice in those years.)

Once in Arkansas, the children's lives become taken up with church and school and helping in the William Johnson General Merchandise Store, referred to by everyone in the community as simply "the Store." Momma has built the business up from a mobile lunch counter for the workers in the area.

The store is the focus of the black community and Marguerite and Bailey get to know everyone, from field hand to lumberman. The children meet Mr. McElroy, an independent black man who "never laughed and seldom smiled, [and] never went to church."[3] Bailey and Marguerite see this as proof of his courage, especially living next door to their religious

Paul Laurence Dunbar was the first African American author to gain national recognition. His writing was a source of inspiration to Angelou.

## PAUL LAURENCE DUNBAR

He was only thirty-three when he died, but from the time Paul Laurence Dunbar was born in 1872 until his death in 1906, he was a keen observer of the world around him. The son of freed slaves, Dunbar reputedly began rhyming words when he was six. Though his parents separated when he was young, he drew on their stories of planation life. He was a master at writing in Southern dialect. But he could write the "King's English," too. Dunbar wrote hundreds of poems and eleven works of prose. In fact, his work has been memorized and recited by countless black Americans, in what one contemporary poet calls a "passing on of literary tradition that occurs within a black family or non-school context."[4]

grandmother. They watch as the obese Reverend H. Thomas takes the choicest parts of Sunday dinner. They survive the depression by bartering with their neighbors, exchanging government issued goods for products in the store, and they do their school work under the watchful eye of their Uncle Willie. Marguerite recalls that it was during the early years in Stamps that she fell in love with Shakespeare, her "first white love and pacified [herself] about his whiteness by saying he had been dead so long it couldn't' matter anymore."[5]

She describes how the field hands start the day full of "laughing, joking, boasting and bragging. One man was going to pick two hundred pounds of cotton, and another three hundred."[6] In the evening, they come back tired and discouraged, carried by big wagons from the "remains of slavery's plantations."[7] Angelou notes how later in her life she would be outraged by the "stereotyped picture of gay sing-songing cotton pickers…I had seen the fingers cut by the mean little

Though slavery had been abolished, many African Americans living in rural areas still worked in the same conditions they had during slavery.

cotton bolls and I had witnessed the backs and shoulders and arms and legs resisting any further demands."[8] It is with observations like these early in the book that Angelou establishes herself as a keen observer and a passionate spokesperson.

### Part II – St. Louis

Without warning, the children's father, Bailey Sr., visits. Not having seen him since they were very small, Maya admits, "We or at any rate I, had built such elaborate fantasies about him, and the illusory mother that seeing him in the flesh shredded my inventions like a hard yank on a paper chain."[9] Still, Maya is proud: "Everyone could tell from the way he talked and the car and clothes that he was rich and maybe had a castle out in California."[10] At the same time, she fears she might not actually be his daughter but rather, an orphan her parents picked out to keep her brother company. Bailey Sr. stays with them in Stamps for three weeks, then announces he must go back to California. Maya is relieved, feeling she can now relax from his constant scrutiny. Then she learns he is taking her and Bailey Jr. with him. At first she is afraid to go, but ultimately squeezes herself in the back of the car despite being emotionally and physically uneasy.

Early on in the drive, Maya realizes her brother is trying to flatter their father and this annoys her. But the real shock is when their father reveals he is driving them to St. Louis to be with their mother, Vivian, and her family, the Baxters. Maya recalls St. Louis as hot, dirty, and crowded. Upon meeting her mother, whom Bailey Jr. will address as Mother Dear, Maya recalls being "struck dumb" and experiencing "love at first sight…My mother's beauty literally assailed me."[11] Her mother wears lipstick; their grandmother had not, believing to do so was a sin. Their mother smiles a lot; their grandmother had not. In almost every way that matters, Momma and Mother are opposites. Angelou the writer reveals her talent for drawing a verbal portrait here. Focusing on physical characteristics, we get a clear sense of what this meeting is like for young Maya, who exists in a world in which she is often uneasy with her physical being: her too black skin, her too nappy hair, her tallness. The description also sets up a tension that foreshadows the tragedy that is to come.

The Baxters are a rough bunch. Grandmother Baxter, who is mostly white, rules the household of six mean children (including Mother Dear) with an iron fist. Equally tough, Grandfather Baxter is known for famously saying: "Bah, Jesus. I live for my wife, my children and my dog."[12] Angelou writes

*I Know Why the Caged Bird Sings* was televised for the first time in 1978.

that during the mid-1930s, their section of town "had all the finesse of a gold-rush town. Prohibition, gambling and all their related vocations were so obviously practiced, that it was hard for me to believe that they were against the law."[13] For the first six months in St. Louis, the children live in their grandparents' home, where numbers runners, gamblers, and bootleggers are frequent visitors. Angelou remembers being fascinated most by her uncles and their meanness. At school, the children excel and are surprised by how little their classmates know. The teachers are much more remote than in Stamps and "talked down to their students from the lofty heights of education and whitefolks' enunciation."[14]

The children's lives are markedly different from what they were in Stamps. Instead of being under the watchful eyes of their grandmother and uncle, and in fact, their entire community in St. Louis, they rarely even see their mother. When they do, it's in a tavern where Mother Dear sings and dances and where they learn to do the "time step" and show off to their mother's friends at the bar. It's a long way from sitting around the store and practicing multiplication tables.

After six months in the Baxter household, Maya and Bailey make another adjustment; this time they move to an apartment with their mother. Though trained as a pediatric nurse, Vivian Baxter makes a living dealing cards. She lives with a man called Mr. Freeman. The children seem to adjust well to city life, but Angelou tells us that she does not consider it home. "I carried the same shield that I had used in Stamps: I didn't come to stay."[15] Interestingly, this is the very same phrase that begins the book—part of the poem Angelou recited at church. In this moment, we understand that they are not just some words Angelou was forced to memorize, but a catchphrase for her life. Up to this point, we have seen Angelou's longing for home and love and stability, but have not known about the defenses, "the shield" she puts up to protect herself. It is as if she does not believe she ever could find "home."

Maya's searching for total acceptance manifests itself in different ways throughout the book. For example, she describes how Bailey develops a stutter and how she is plagued with nightmares so that Vivian brings Maya into bed with her and Mr. Freeman.

One morning her mother gets up early, leaving Maya alone with Mr. Freeman. Freeman uses the opportunity to involve her in his masturbation, which confuses and at the same time comforts Maya, because afterwards "[h]e held me so softly that I wished he wouldn't ever let me go. I felt at home."[16] But Freeman also threatens Angelou: if she tells anyone, he says, he will kill Bailey. Ironically, when the situation is most dangerous, she says she feels at home. This is something she has not been able to experience so far in her life, especially in St. Louis, which she has told us feels like a foreign country.

At this point Bailey and Maya are more distant from one another. Angelou describes spending days at the library alone and unbothered. However, her encounters with Freeman are not over. We learn that he rapes her, after which she faints. Freeman warns her to remain quiet, sending her off to the library after the rape. Angelou describes trying to get there, feeling "the wet in my pants" and her hips which felt as though they were "coming out of the sockets."[17] Confused, she wanders around until she returns home and goes straight to bed.

Bailey and Vivian notice something is wrong, but Maya says nothing. Mr. Freeman hovers menacingly in her bedroom doorway. Later at night, Angelou hears her mother and Freeman arguing and fears he will do something to her mother. In the morning, Maya learns that Mr. Freeman has moved out. She wonders whether it might now be all right to explain what happened, but is afraid that Bailey will blame her and no longer love her. Without saying why, she begs him to take her away from St. Louis. In her anguish, Maya has perspired so much, the bed sheets are wet and need changing. Vivian and Bailey find a blood-stained pair of underpants that she has hidden under the mattress. She is taken to the hospital, where Bailey pleads with her to tell him who has hurt her. When Maya insists that it must remain a secret or Bailey will be killed, he convinces her that will not happen. Unable to contain the secret anymore, she tells Bailey.

Freeman is arrested and Maya is required to face him in court. Her thuggish uncles are present, as are her brother, her mother, and grandmother. When questioned about the number of times Freeman has made advances, Maya lies and say it was only once. She tells us that she does this because she is fearful. She believes that her uncles will kill *her*, that her grandmother will stop speaking to her and that her mother will be disappointed in her. Worst of all, she believes Bailey will stop loving her because she's kept such a big secret from him. Even as she tells the lie, it "lumped in my throat and I couldn't get air."[18]

Freeman is convicted, but his lawyer gets him out of jail on a technicality the very same day. In the afternoon, a policeman arrives at the Baxter home where Maya is playing and delivers the news that Mr. Freeman has been found dead. Grandmother Baxter appears to be sympathetic, but once the policeman leaves, admonishes the children never to speak of the incident or "that evil man" again. As readers, we can guess that someone in the Baxter clan had something to do with Freeman's death. Maya certainly feels responsible by lying.

"Even Christ Himself turned His back on Satan. Wouldn't He turn His back on me? I could feel the evilness flowing through my body and waiting, pent up to rush off my tongue if I tried to open my mouth."[19] Believing that her words have the power kill to the people she loves, Maya decides to stop talking.

At first the family accepts this. But once the doctor says she is healed, everyone expects her to return to her former self. When Maya does not, she is accused of being uppity and is eventually thrashed by any relative who feels offended by her behavior. Angelou writes: "There is nothing more appalling than a constantly morose child."[20] Her words are certainly insincere, since the girl could hardly be expected to process the violence done to her in a matter of weeks. But most likely, the dishonesty is intentional, a device by which Angelou underscores how different she is from her mother and her kinfolk in St. Louis. In any case, at the end of chapter 13, Angelou informs us that she and Bailey are being sent back to Stamps.

### Part III – Back to Stamps

Chapter 14 begins with Angelou's observation that the "barrenness of Stamps was exactly what I wanted."[21] Gone is the noise and bustle of St. Louis. Instead, nothing ever happens and Angelou describes the feeling that she is creeping into a cocoon. On the other hand, in Stamps the children have the status of celebrities, having been carried off by their father with his big-city accent and fancy car. Bailey enjoys the attention and brags about the tallness of the buildings, the hugeness of the watermelon, the deepness of the snow. For her part, Maya continues to say nothing. The people in Stamps accept this, while Maya tells us that she has difficulty seeing colors and hearing sounds. "People's names escaped me and I began to worry over my sanity."[22]

After almost a year of silence, Maya meets "the lady who threw me my first life line."[23] Her name is Mrs. Flowers, "the aristocrat of black Stamps." And though she is different in just about every way from Momma, the two women seem to be close friends. Angelou is embarrassed when Momma uses improper grammar around Mrs. Flowers and is mortified when Mrs. Flowers compliments Momma's sewing and Momma lifts Maya's dress over her head to show the woman. In a display of her gentility, Mrs. Flowers tries to keep Momma from pulling the dress off completely.

Mrs. Flowers asks Maya to walk her home and carry her groceries. (Angelou tells us that any other black woman in town would be expected to carry her own items.) On the way, Mrs. Flowers remarks that she knows Maya's written work is excellent but that teachers have trouble getting her to talk in class. Perhaps she has heard this from town gossip or perhaps Momma has told her in an attempt to get Mrs. Flowers to help Maya speak again. In any case, Mrs. Flowers says that Maya doesn't have to talk, but that what separates man from other life is this ability. Mrs. Flowers also says she knows Maya reads a lot, but that written words are nothing without the human voice to "infuse them with the shades of deeper meaning."[24] Maya is enchanted by their talk as well as by the woman's home. Mrs. Flowers gives Maya a book to take home and asks that she come back having picked a poem to memorize and recite.

Maya rushes home, excited. "I was liked and what a difference it made. I was respected, not as Mrs. Henderson's grandchild or Bailey's sister, but for just being Marguerite Johnson."[25] Back at home, Maya is excited to share her experience with Bailey, along with some cookies Mrs. Flowers has made and given Maya to take home. To Bailey, Maya remarks, "By the way, Bailey, Mrs. Flowers sent you some tea cookies."[26] Hearing this, Momma becomes angry and hits her with a switch; Momma thinks that Maya has taken Jesus's name in vain. This incident is significant, underscoring the difference between the world Maya is attracted to and the world of her family. The fact that her grandmother most likely played a role in Mrs. Flowers and Maya meeting suggests the possibility that these worlds might meet and converge.

In contrast, chapter 16 begins with an anecdote about the world of white privilege. Angelou mentions a white woman she knows who would "quickly describe herself as a liberal."[27] This woman labels Maya a débutante because of Momma's standing in their community, but as Angelou points out, this misses the point. Young women of color did get an education for their future, but it was all about how to make ends meet and reckon with an uncertain future.

Angelou goes on to tell how when she is ten, she works for a white woman, who insists on calling her Mary. Furious and insulted, Maya tells Bailey and the two come up with a plan to get back at the woman. The next time Maya is working, when the woman calls her "Mary," Maya drops a favorite piece of china and continues to drop glass and crockery. When the woman's friend asks whether "Mary" did this, the woman yells, "Her name is Margaret, god damn it!"[28] This vignette serves a dual purpose: first, it is in sharp contrast to the rich and refined life of Mrs. Flowers, a black aristocrat. It is as if Angelou is underscoring the hollowness of the white so-called gentry. Second, it is the first time in the narrative that Maya actually stands up for herself, accenting the seminal themes of identity and self-worth.

The focus shifts to Bailey in chapter 17. One night he is late coming home from the movies. This is worrisome, Angelou tells us in a poignant aside, because "[t]he Black woman in the South who raises sons, grandsons and nephews had her heartstrings tied to a hanging noose. Any break from routine may herald for them unbearable news."[29] After Uncle Willie switches Bailey for worrying the family, he remains remote. Finally he reveals to Angelou that he saw their mother in a movie. He explains that it wasn't actually her but the actress looked so much like their mother, he stayed to watch the movie a second time. Angelou realizes she cannot say anything to Momma or Uncle Willie. "She was our mother and belonged to us," Angelou writes. "She was never mentioned to anyone because we simply didn't have enough of her to share."[30]

In the next chapter, Angelou returns her focus to the store and the exhausted workers who return when the day is over. Their shoulders droop, their palms slip, and their minds sag. Maya confesses to hating them all for letting themselves be overworked and pretending things are not bad. One man mentions a revival meeting, which Maya cannot believe any of the workers would dream of going to after such a hard day: "Go to church in that cloud of weariness? Not go home and lay those tortured bones in a father bed? The idea came to me that my people may be a race of masochists and that not only was it our fate to live the poorest, roughest life, but that we liked it like that."[31]

Maya finds the proceedings at the revival shocking. It is held in a tent, not a church, and the crowd is from all different denominations: Baptists, Methodists, and Episcopalians. The minister preaches from a wobbling altar not about what charity is, but what it is *not*. It is not about expecting thanks when you give someone a job, or about expecting him to call you master when he delivers an honest day's work. Nor does charity make a person feel unimportant and belittled. "In short, charity is not about the things white people do."[32] He tells the people gathered in the tent that they will enjoy blissful eternity for all their worldly suffering. Maya notices the worshipers are temporarily energized, but as the revival winds down, "Reality began its tedious crawl back into their reasoning. After all, they were needy and hungry and despised and dispossessed."[33]

Following the revival meeting, we read of another triumph for the black community in Stamps. Angelou describes the boxing match between Joe Louis and Italian boxer Primo Carnera. In Stamps, the community comes together at the store to listen on the radio. What's important here is not so much who Louis is fighting, but the fact that his opponent is white. Angelou writes that when Louis seems to be losing, "It was another lynching, yet another Black man hanging on a tree."[34] When Louis gains the upper hand and wins the match, the community in Stamps feels it: "Champion of the world. A Black boy. Some Black mother's son. He was the strongest man in the world." But again, the victory is short-lived, and the reality of being a person of color in Stamps, Arkansas sets in. Angelou writes "Those who lived too far had made arrangements to stay in town. It wouldn't do for a Black man and his family to be caught on a lonely country road on a night when Joe Louis had proved that we were the strongest people in the world."[35]

In the next several chapters, Maya describes making a friend her own age, her brother's burgeoning sexuality, and experiencing the realities of death when a neighbor dies and she must attend the funeral. We also see her transform from the withdrawn and guarded soul she was when she returned to Stamps, to a smart and cheerful graduate of the eighth grade class of the Lafayette County Training School. Momma is making her dress and the description of it could not be more different from the one in the beginning of the book: "I was going to be lovely. A walking model of all the various styles of fine hand sewing."[36] She smiles so much her jaw aches. Even

Champion boxer Joe Louis was a source of ethnic pride for many African Americans in the 1930s and 1940s.

her hair, she writes, "had lengthened and thickened so it kept at last to its braided pattern."[37]

But again, Maya's happiness is not destined to last. At the last minute, the program is revised to accommodate a speaker who must "speak and run;" a white man who announces all the changes that are coming to white schools in the district. He contends that he's spoken to people at a very high level about all the athletic talent at Lafayette County Training School. "The white kids were going to have a chance to become Galileos and Madame Curies and Edisons and Gauguins and our boys (the girls weren't even in on it) would try to be Jesse Owenses and Joe Louises," observes Angelou.[38] Outraged, she questions why whites get to make these kinds of pronouncements. Of course Owens and Louis were great heroes, but so were George Washington Carver and Vivien Thomas. For Maya, the ceremony is ruined and she cannot pay attention. And then a remarkable thing happens: the valedictorian, Henry Reed, turns his back to the audience and leads his classmates in "Lift Ev'ry Voice and Sing" (also known as the "Negro National Anthem). Writes Angelou: "Our mothers and fathers stood in the dark hall and joined the hymn of encouragement...Every child I knew had learned that song with his ABCs."[39] Instead of a feeling of disgust, Angelou records being proud of her blackness, a feeling that will be sustained through the rest of the book and played out in the way Maya Angelou continued to lead her life.

Several months later, another clash occurs between blacks and whites. Maya develops a toothache and, breaking with convention, Momma takes her to the white dentist, assuming that he will treat the child because he owes Momma money. The dentist makes them wait at his back door for over an hour, then refuses to help and makes a racist remark. Momma asks

## Joe Louis—Brown Bomber

Joseph Louis Barrow was born in Lafayette, Alabama, in 1914. He spent his formative years there, but when relatives moved north and reported that there were jobs, Louis's family migrated to Detroit. When he was about twelve, he moved there as well.

Louis dropped out of high school and began to work in an automobile plant. He developed an interest in boxing and spent his free time practicing. Soon, he was training as a full-time boxer under the name Joe Louis. He quickly rose to become the national amateur light heavyweight champion. After that, he fought as a professional with Julian Black and John Roxborough as managers and Jack Blackburn as trainer. He earned the heavyweight championship title by defeating James Braddock on June 22, 1937. One of his most memorable wins, however, was against Max Schmeling, a German boxer who the Nazis touted as the Aryan ideal. Though Louis lost to him in 1936, two years later he claimed victory by knocking Schmeling to the ground in the first round.

In general, most African Americans felt the way Angelou did. They were proud of Louis, especially at a time when the white public barely credited African American athletes. They were proud of Louis's public persona: his love for his family and clean living. Any transgressions from this behavior were never widely reported, and Louis managed to remain a grateful son who gave full credit to his mother for his success. African-American fans, for their part, interpreted his victories personally, recognizing him as a talented figure, ready to make sacrifices to achieve specific goals.

Maya to wait while she speaks with the dentist privately. As she waits, Maya imagines the scene inside: her grandmother commanding the room, the dentist helpless and shaking, Momma turning the dentist's assistant into a sack of chicken feed on her way out. What actually transpires is that Momma is able to force the dentist to give her bus fare for them to get to the black dentist in Texarkana—not exactly what she was going for but also not a total loss.

We learn some important lessons from this account. First, Momma does what is necessary, especially when it concerns her granddaughter. Though she prefers not to deal with the white people in town, she does it, giving us a further indication of her intelligence and tenacity. When they get back to Stamps, we hear Momma tell Uncle Willie how she was able to get the uppity Dr. Lincoln to give her the money: "He said, 'Annie I done tole you, I aint gonna mess around in no niggah's mouth.' I said, 'Somebody go to do it then,' and he said, 'Take her to Texarkana to the colored dentist' and that's when I said, 'If you paid me the money I could afford to take her.' He said 'It's all been paid.' I tole him everything but the interest had been paid. He said, ''Twasn't no interest.' I said, ''Tis now.'...Even though by rights he was paid up before, I figger, he gonna be that kind of nasty, he gonna pay for it."[40] Maya remarks that she likes her imagined version of events better. Some critics conjecture that Angelou's preference for the fantastical is really a way of using creativity and imagination to avoid racism and victimization.

It is at this point in the autobiography that Momma announces she will be taking the children to California. Writes Angelou, "Whatever the real reason, the Truth for taking us to California, I shall always think it lay mostly in an incident in which Bailey had the leading part."[41] Bailey had come home one afternoon shaking with his little face "no longer black, but a dirty colorless gray." He had seen a dead black man dragged from a pond. A white man had ordered him and some other black bystanders to help carry the bloated, rotting body to the nearby jail. Once there the white man had pretended he was going to lock the corpse, Bailey, and the other men in with the black prisoners. In Angelou's recollection Bailey says, "They called the white man 'Boss.' They said, 'boss, surely we ain't done nothing bad enough for you to put another nigger in here with us, and a dead one at that.' Then they laughed. They all laughed like there was something funny."[42] Angelou notes that at this point, Bailey is "locked in the enigma that young Southern Black boys start to unravel, start to *try* to unravel, from seven years old to death. The humorless puzzle of inequality and hate."[43] He looks to his uncle and grandmother for an explanation, but they seem to have no real answers.

### Part IV—California

World War II is beginning and San Francisco is booming. Momma brings Maya (Bailey will follow a month later) to her mother in Los Angeles. Occasionally, Maya's father visits. Momma stays with Maya until she and her mother move upstate to Oakland, about six months after their arrival in Los Angeles. Angelou makes an interesting observation about this: "Years had to pass before I reflected on Momma's remarkable adjustment to that foreign life. An old Southern Negro woman who had lived her life under the left breast of her community learned to deal with white landlords, Mexican neighbors and Negro strangers."[44] The passage goes on to describe how Momma negotiates the big stores and different accents, reminding us of the startling contrast between the

Deep South and the West, and once again underscoring the kind of remarkable force Angelou's grandmother was.

Once Bailey arrives and the apartment in Oakland is ready, Momma departs. For Maya, this creates some nervousness: "There were foggy days of unknowing for Bailey and me. It was all well and good to say we would be with our parents, but after all, who were they?"[45] Apparently Vivian Baxter is nervous too, a fact that Bailey and Maya are aware of. In Oakland, they go to school but no one in the family asks them about it. They find out that their mother and her business partner (and Angelou speculates he may have been more than

Though it can hardly compare with traffic today, downtown Los Angeles was bustling in the late 1940s.

that) had a fight that ended with him punching Vivian and her shooting him.

The United States has now entered into World War II. Maya recalls people shouting in the streets, "We're at war. We've declared war on Japan," while Grandmother Baxter assures her that President Roosevelt will know how to keep the nation from being bombed. At the same time, Vivian Baxter marries Daddy Clidell, a successful businessman who would turn out to be the first true father Maya would know. Bailey, Maya, and her mother move with him to San Francisco. As the streets empty of Japanese citizens, Maya notices that their businesses are replaced by "enterprising Negro businessmen"[46] whose patrons are the Southern blacks recruited to work in ammunitions factories and shipyards. The part of San Francisco known as the Western Addition, which before the war had been the Japanese area, "became San Francisco's Harlem."

Maya notices the indifference blacks feel toward the Japanese and speculates why: "The chance to live in two or three story apartment buildings (which became instant slums), and to earn two and even three-figured weekly checks, was blinding. For the first time he could think of himself as a Boss, a Spender. He was able to pay people to work for him."[47] According to Angelou, this prosperity was such a reversal for most black people that they were reluctant to let it go or to consider at what cost their fortunes had come. Angelou also suggests the indifference of the blacks stems from racism: "The Japanese were not whitefolks. Their eyes, language and customs belied the white skin and proved to their dark successors that since they didn't have to be feared, neither did they have to be considered."[48]

Ironically, Maya feels at home amid the chaos: "The air of collective displacement, the impermanence of life in wartime and the gauche personalities of the more recent arrivals tended to dissipate my own sense of not belonging. In San Francisco, for the first time, I perceived myself as part of something."[49] But she also knows that beneath the surface, and despite the temporary anti-Asian sentiments, prejudice against blacks remains. "San Franciscans would have sworn on the Golden Gate Bridge that racism was missing from the heart of their air-conditioned city. But they would have been sadly mistaken."[50]

In Chapter 28, we learn that Maya is now in high school. At first she has trouble settling and is transferred to a school in which she is one of only three black students. The neighborhood is strikingly different from her own and she reports coming to appreciate her background more as she rides the streetcar to school. In this school, she is not the smartest or the most fearless. Her white classmates "never hesitated to hold up their hands in response to a teacher's question; even when they were wrong they were wrong aggressively."[51] By contrast, she feels she must be absolutely certain of herself before opening her mouth. She is offered a scholarship to the California Labor School, which offers night classes to adults and alongside them she takes dance and drama.

Maya then moves attention to Daddy Clidell, a man she describes as successful despite his lack of education: "He was a simple man who had no inferiority complex about his lack of education and, even more amazing, no superiority complex because he had succeeded despite that lack."[52] And though he introduces her to con men and teaches her to play high stakes card games, there is something fundamentally decent about him. Angelou's focus on her surrogate father is in sharp contrast to her actual father, with whom she interacts in the next chapter. Bailey Sr. invites her to visit him in Southern

California during the summer. At first she is "jumpy with excitement"[53] but that excitement soon fades to disappointment as she sees her father's home (a trailer in a secluded trailer park) and a girlfriend not much older than she is. Maya and the girlfriend almost instantly dislike each other—Maya's father has told his girlfriend that his children are nine and ten—a fact that Bailey Sr. seems to delight in.

In a surprising move, Bailey Sr. suggests that just he and Maya take a day trip to Mexico without his girlfriend. Apparently, he does this often to pick up food and make special

## Japanese Internment

After the attack on Pearl Harbor (December 7, 1941), Americans succumbed to fear, distrust, and political suggestion and required the forced removal of all Japanese Americans to internment camps. Though many of the Japanese immigrants had been in the United States for generations, they were accustomed to the prejudice.

Between 1942 and 1945, there were ten camps, holding approximately 120,000 Japanese Americans for varying periods of time in California, Arizona, Wyoming, Colorado, Utah, and Arkansas. The rationale for moving Japanese Americans was concern that they were involved in espionage and sabotage.

Life in the camps was not pleasant. Most were uninsulated barracks containing only cots and coal-burning stoves. Residents used common bathroom and laundry facilities, but hot water was usually limited. The camps were surrounded by barbed-wire fences patrolled by armed guards. As most of the internees were given an average of two weeks to get their affairs in order, people were forced to sell some or all of their property, including businesses, and bring only what they could carry.

One of the most well-known internment camps, Manzanar, housed roughly ten thousand people who tried to continue their daily lives while in confinement.

meals. Since he has not made much of an attempt to be with her since her arrival, Maya is excited by the prospect. Once over the border, they are stopped by some kind of guard. Her father stops to drink and chat with the man, apparently fluent in Spanish. At one point, Maya, who understands most of the conversation, realizes that he is offering her to the guard for marriage. Eventually they drive off, but this is clearly not the expedition Maya had imagined. They pass through steep mountains on twisting roads arriving "in the dirt yard of a cantina where half-clothed children chased mean-looking chickens around and around."[54] Here, it appears Maya's father is well-known, and after a short while, Maya relaxes and enjoys herself.

After a few hours, however, Maya realizes she hasn't seen her father. At first, she panics, thinking she has been abandoned. But she finds his car outside the cantina and decides to wait there. When he finally reappears, he is thoroughly drunk. Maya commandeers him into the car, where he falls asleep in the back seat. So it is she, who has never driven in her life, who gets behind the wheel. She makes it to the guard station before crashing into another car. "Fear was absent from my sensations. I wondered in this order: was I hurt, was anyone else hurt, would I go to jail, what where the Mexicans saying and finally, had Dad awakened."[55] Her father remains asleep and Maya and the passengers from the car she crashed into "began the herculean job of waking Dad."[56] Maya remains oddly calm, watching "coolly as the remaining people paraded, making figure eights around me and their badly bruised automobile."[57] Once her father is awake, he asks Maya for the car's insurance papers, grabs a half-empty bottle of liquor, and heads off with the guard and the driver of the other car. A few minutes later, the three return laughing and Bailey Sr. gets behind the wheel and drives the rest of the way to California. Maya is angry that she gets no credit from her father for her accomplishment: her toughness and her quick mastery of driving. Instead he acts indifferent and they "drove into the city in a cold and private silence."[58]

As soon as they walk in the door, Bailey Sr.'s girlfriend, Dolores, begins an argument. She says he has let Maya come between them. The fight intensifies, ending with Bailey Sr. leaving with a slam of the door. Though Maya does not like Dolores, she feels sorry for her and tries to console her by telling her she has no intention of coming between the two. Dolores responds unkindly, admonishing her for eavesdropping and then escalating matters by calling Maya's mother a whore. At this point, Maya slaps Dolores and Dolores reacts by trying to knife her. Even as the exchange is happening, Maya reports, "Maybe if I had been older, or had had my mother longer, or understood Dolores' frustration more deeply, my response would not have been so violent."[59] Maya understands the precariousness of her relationship with her mother and of the fragile nature of her own feelings as she continues, "I know that the awful accusation struck not so much at my filial love as at the foundation of my new existence. If there was a chance of truth to the charge, I would not be able to live, to continue to live with Mother, and I so wanted to."[60] Once again, Angelou is vulnerable, questioning who she is and where she belongs.

Maya stumbles outside, realizing that she is bleeding. Dolores comes after her screaming, this time with a hammer in her hands. Maya heads for her father's car as her father and the neighbors he was visiting run into the yard. Bailey Sr. talks Dolores back into the trailer, then returns angrily to the car. Bailey Sr. begins to drive and Maya, assuming they are going to a hospital, begins fantasizing about her death and to whom she will bequeath her things. To her surprise and dismay, her father drives her to a friend's house, where her wound is cleaned and bandaged. Her father explains that he cannot have people learning about the shameful incident: "He was after all a Mason, an Elk, a naval dietitian, and the first Negro deacon in the Lutheran Church. No Negro in the city would be able to hold his head up if our misfortune became common knowledge."[61]

Bailey Sr. then drives her to another friend's where she is to stay for the night. She wakes up to empty and unfamiliar surroundings and makes herself breakfast. Her father returns on his way to work, gives her some money, a kiss, and says he'll be back later. Maya weighs her options: She doesn't want to stay in the empty and unfamiliar place. She considers that if she were to disappear, her father and his girlfriend would be happy. She wonders if she has the nerve to commit suicide. She thinks of her brother and hears him counseling her to leave. "But don't kill yourself," she imagines him saying, "You can always do that if things get bad enough."[62] So Maya makes herself a few sandwiches, takes a supply of fresh bandages, and leaves. Realizing that she cannot go home just yet because her mother would notice her wound, Maya wanders around. Eventually she finds a junkyard with old cars, one of which she decides to sleep in. She notices that despite the uncertainty of her situation, she feels a sense of freedom. "I was a loose kite in a gentle wind floating with only my will for an anchor."[63] She falls asleep by counting the headlights of oncoming cars.

In the morning, Maya learns the junkyard is inhabited by a group of teens who have formed a kind of community. They have rules such as no members of the opposite sex sleeping together, and no stealing because it will alert the police and they are all underage. Everyone has a job, be it bottle collecting, lawn mowing, or running errands for people in the community. Maya stays with them for a month and learns new skills, like how to actually drive and dance. But even more important, she is accepted for herself. Ironically, it is in the absence of any adults and without a real home that Maya truly learns self-reliance.

At the end of a month, Maya calls her mother and asks for a plane ticket home. Interestingly, there is no great fanfare. The teens at the junkyard seem unmoved by the announcement that she is leaving. Nor does her mother seem to realize that she has not been with Bailey Sr. the whole time. Instead, Vivian notes Maya's lean and unkempt look and tells her she needs to eat more.

Settling in after her summer isn't easy for Maya. Her San Francisco home seems "smaller and quieter after the trip south and the first bloom of San Francisco's glamour had dulled around the edges."[64] Maya is a far cry from the girl who began the book wishing to be transformed into a white fairy princess. She has changed in a much more profound way. No longer her naïve self, she is more comfortable in her own skin. At the same time, her brother, Bailey, is changing too. No longer under their mother's spell, Bailey asserts his independence with hip new friends and late nights out. One night, after a particularly heated argument with Vivian, Bailey heads off with some of his things to stay with a friend. In the morning Maya finds him and learns that despite appearances, Bailey and Vivian have spoken, that their mother understands his need for independence, and is arranging for him to get a job as a dining car waiter on the Southern Pacific Railway. Bailey is confident that he will do well enough at the job to get a promotion and eventually move up the ranks in the railway. Interestingly, the job will require a lot of travel and the sort of moving around that Maya has been trying to avoid most of her life.

As if she has been preparing us for this moment, Maya has not mentioned her brother in the last few chapters. Now they are discussing a very real separation as the two try to find their own way in the world. And it seems they will have to do it without each other. Maya realizes she cannot go back to living her life as she had before. Even though she is only fifteen, she decides to get a job, something she knows her mother will approve of. The job she chooses is streetcar conductor. When her mother tells her there are no blacks working on the cars, Maya decides to fight for the job and to do it on her own terms. This situation is different from the time in Stamps when she rebelled against her white employer by breaking dishes. That had been Bailey's scheme. Now Maya has the opportunity to control her own fate and build her self-image. As critics have commented, "this event fits with the slave narrative tradition, in which a confrontation with the oppressor occurs and there is a drive to achieve order out of chaos."[65]

Maya arrives at the San Francisco Transit Authority offices and says she is responding to the ad in that morning's *Chronicle*. The receptionist who greets her tries to find ways to discourage her, telling her that they are only accepting applications from candidates who come through an agency and that the hiring manager is not there. But Maya suspects racism. She writes: "The miserable little encounter had nothing to do with me, the me of me, any more than it had to do with that silly clerk. The incident was a recurring dream concocted years before by stupid whites and it eternally came back to haunt us all." So Angelou can forgive the receptionist as "a fellow victim of the same puppeteer."[66] What she cannot do is give up. She appeals to various black organizations and government offi-

## Black Railway Workers

African Americans have a long history with the railroad. As slaves, they constructed most of the South's 8,784-mile (14,136-km) rail network. They operated trains as firemen, brakemen, and switchmen. And they loaded and unloaded freight cars. Many of these jobs were dirty and dangerous. But there was one job that was perhaps more coveted: the Pullman porter.

Before the Civil War, African Americans had been given servant roles on passenger train cars. Enslaved men who worked the trains as firemen or brakemen were sometimes called upon to help passengers on and off trains, carry luggage, get water for the thirsty, and keep oil lamps full and the stove stoked. Soon after the war, ex-slaves represented a huge labor pool. Their freedom coincided with the fortunes of George Mortimer Pullman, the man who invented the Pullman car, a train car designed for passengers to sleep in as they began traveling longer and longer distances by rail.

Working the sleeping car was not easy. A porter typically made up berths, carried pails of drinking water, prepared and sold meals and coffee, and walked up and down many cars selling newspapers, magazines, candy, and fruit. They tended coal-burning stoves at the end of each car, and at the end of each journey they cleaned the cars. But as the number of freed slaves multiplied, plenty of African Americans were willing to trade cotton picking and farming for any other form of employment.

George Pullman knew that his white customers would like black servants waiting on them. He recognized that many were not wealthy enough to keep servants at home. He wasn't just selling a train ride, he was selling the service as well.

In the beginning, porters did not get wages. The money they made was from tips or from selling food. That changed in the 1920s when the Federal Transportation Act forced the Pullman Company to allow unions. The result was the Brotherhood of Sleeping Car Porters, the first African American controlled union in the United States. In 1926, there were 20,244 African American porters. They worked an average of four hundred hours a month and were paid approximately $66. The union worked for years to improve the hours, the wages, and the working conditions for the African American railway workers.

cials and gets nowhere. At the point where Maya questions her resolve, she tells us that she and her mother "began our first steps on the long path toward mutual adult admiration."[67] Her mother never nags, but advises her to put her entire self into whatever cause she chooses, pray, and then be patient. "She had a store of aphorisms which she dished out as the occasion demanded. Strangely, as bored as I was with clichés, her inflection gave them something new, and set me thinking for a little while at least."[68]

How she finally lands the job, Maya does not know. What she does know is that she gets the most undesirable shifts. There is also a change in the way she feels about riding into

In 1944, Angelou became the first black cable car conductor in San Francisco.

the more affluent areas of town. "I lost some of my need for the Black ghetto's shielding-sponge quality," she informs us.[69] She works for only a semester before returning to school full time. Here again, she feels like a misfit. "Within weeks, I realized that my schoolmates and I were on paths moving diametrically away from each other."[70] While they worry about football games and who to nominate for student president, Maya recalls her near disastrous trip down a Mexican mountain and her summer in a junkyard commune. She says "Without willing it, I had gone from being ignorant of being ignorant to be aware of being aware."[71] In an observation that foreshadows what is to come, Maya tells us that she is an adult: "The command to grow up at once was more bearable than the faceless horror of wavering purpose, which was youth."[72] She goes on to explain that sudden maturity is not unusual for young black women: "The Black female is assaulted in her tender years by all those common forces of nature at the same time that she is caught in the tripartite crossfire of masculine prejudice, white illogical hate and Black lack of power."[73]

We are now close to the end of the first autobiography and it seems Angelou has circled back to her unhappiness with her body. Concerned that she is not feminine enough, she reveals that she wonders whether she is a lesbian. Though she looks for information in books, she turns to her mother and even though the two have grown closer, the conversation feels awkward, harkening back to conversations Angelou records earlier in her narrative.

Convinced that she will never have a boyfriend unless she agrees to have sex, Maya begins casting around. She chooses her most handsome classmate and propositions him. He accepts. "Even as the scene was being enacted, I realized the imbalance in his values. He thought I was giving him something and the fact of the matter was it was my intention to take something from him."[74] Maya goes on to say that the boy is so conceited he can't possibly understand what she is doing. Of course, the act is not intimate and even though at this point, Maya has experienced a lot, she still does not connect how true emotional involvement might yield to that "moonlight-on-the-prairie feeling."[75] Nor does it help her answer questions about her sexuality. What does happen is that Maya becomes pregnant.

We have reached the final chapter of the book. As it opens, Maya tells of a mix of emotions: fear, guilt, and a bit of self-loathing. Reeling with these emotions, she sends a letter to Bailey (who we learn is now overseas with the merchant marine). He advises her not to tell Daddy Clidell and Vivian because they will want her to quit school. He fears if she does that, she will never go back. Maya manages to keep her pregnancy a secret until after high school graduation, when she writes Daddy Clidell and Vivian a note. The adults respond with surprise that she has been able to keep a secret, but there is no judgment or condemnation on their part.

The delivery is easy and Maya's son is born. She confesses that at this point, "just as gratefulness was confused in my mind with love, so possession became mixed up with motherhood."[76] As a teen and a first-time mother, Maya is fearful that she might somehow hurt her newborn. Recognizing this, her mother insists that she and her three-week-old son sleep in the same bed. Maya dozes off and is woken by a shake on her shoulder. It is her mother, commanding her to look at the baby. Maya assumes the worst, until she sees that her son has moved but that she too has moved to cradle around him. Her mother reflects, "See you don't have to think about doing the right thing. If you're for the right thing, then you do it without thinking."[77]

## Themes

### Coming of Age

In many respects, *I Know Why the Caged Bird Sings* can be seen as a coming of age story, documenting Angelou's passage from childhood to young adulthood. In fact, some critics have suggested that this is why Angelou's work has such universal

Angelou and her son, Guy, were very close. Both writers, they shared the stage at the National Black Arts Festival in 2005, where this picture was taken.

appeal: she writes candidly about experiences all of us go through. Some critics have noted that all of the positive role models in the autobiography are women: her mother, her grandmother, and Mrs Flowers. The men in the book, aside from Bailey Jr., are weak or stand in the way of Angelou's success: Mr. Freeman, Uncle Willie (who is actually physically weak), even her own father. These critics suggest that Angelou is writing not so much about herself as about "an archetypal 'self' demonstrating the trials, rejections, and endurances which so many Black women share."[78] According to literary scholar Sondra O'Neale, Angelou's autobiography is not the product of egotism. Rather it is Angelou's revelation that "she is because her life is an inextricable part of the misunderstood reality of who Black people and Black women truly are."[79]

### The American Dream and the Great Migration

Fifty years after slavery was outlawed, many Southern blacks were barely scratching out a living. Some were still picking cotton for white landowners, and in time, when machinery replaced people, even that source of income dissolved. African Americans began to move North in large numbers in a movement called the Great Migration in an attempt to find economic and social prosperity, to become part of the American Dream. And they hoped to escape Southern racism. So-called Jim Crow laws, which allowed racial segregation in every aspect of life, had sprung up around the country and were particularly pernicious in the southern states. For example, these laws required blacks to pay taxes and take literacy tests so they could vote. The laws forbade interracial marriages and prevented blacks from buying or renting property in white neighborhoods. They required blacks to attend separate schools and to sit in separate areas of restaurants and public transportation. Though a blatant violation of the civil rights guaranteed to black Americans in post–Civil War America, the laws were sanctioned by the US Supreme Court when they upheld the doctrine of "separate but equal" in the 1896 court case *Plessy v. Ferguson*.

"For Angelou, in *I Know Why the Caged Bird Sings*, the American Dream is somewhere over the bridge in the white part of town," writes critic Diane Telgen.[80] But gradually,

## *Plessy v. Ferguson*

In 1892, a man named Homer Plessy deliberately broke a law that prohibited white and black Americans from occupying the same train car. This act of civil disobedience had been organized by the New Orleans Citizen's Committee. Fed up with laws that masked their true discriminatory nature, the group intended to take the case all the way to the Supreme Court. Plessy was light skinned and able to pass as white. He bought a ticket for the "whites only" section, then announced to the conductor that he was black. When the conductor asked him to move, Plessy refused and was arrested.

Plessy's attorney, presiding in front of district court judge John Ferguson, argued that the "Separate Car Act" violated both the Thirteenth and Fourteenth Amendments. However, Ferguson ruled against Plessy (1896) in a decision that maintained "separate WAS equal," thus reinforcing the practice of racial segregation. It has been called one of the nineteenth century's most important decisions concerning the meaning of the Thirteen and Fourteenth Amendments. The ruling allowed southern states to legally segregate on the basis of race and deny black Americans their civil rights. The ruling would not be overturned until 1954 with another case, *Brown v. Board of Education*.

Angelou sees that the dream is not without its flaws. During her struggle to become a street car conductor, Angelou is quick to let us know that while none of the whites she knows in San Francisco would consider themselves racist, their racism is, in fact, just more covert. In time, she learns to feel comfortable outside the black neighborhoods in town and triumphs over both snobbish whites and pretentious blacks.

## Writing Style

As an autobiography, *I Know Why the Caged Bird Sings* uses first-person narration. However, much of the writing is filtered. First we see people, places, and events as the young Marguerite sees them, and later as Maya the teen does. We see her transform from an awkward young girl into a determined and wise-for-her-years young adult.

## Narration

Narration is key to this work. By using first person, we have direct access to Marguerite/Maya's thoughts and problems. But we can only learn what Angelou chooses to tell us about her surroundings and the people she interacts with. And it is through the lens of her assumptions that we learn about things. So in some sense, the work is slanted. But of course, this is the point of an autobiography: to present the experiences and impressions of a specific individual.

## Setting

Angelou describes many places and times: St. Louis and the deep South in the 1930s and 40s, and California in the 1950s. By the end of *I Know Why the Caged Bird Sings* we feel that Angelou has come to some revelation about who she is and how she fits into the world. Later autobiographies will inform us about how Angelou fares on her road to self-discovery.

Unlike other authors of color (Richard Wright, for example), Angelou is more focused on her interior landscape. Literary critic Stephen Butterfield notes that *I Know Why the Caged Bird Sings* "is not really [about] the struggle of the bird; it is the exploration of the cage, the gradual discovery of its boundaries, the loosening of certain bars, that she can slip through when the keepers' backs are turned."[81] While Angelou deals with whites because she must, "her happiness, sorrows, lessons, meanings, self-confidence, seem to come from within her private circle of light. Part of her is always untouched by the oppression, observing and commenting on it from a distance."[82]

## Allusion

An allusion is a reference to an event, person, place, or artistic work which the writer does not necessarily explain, but rather assumes that the reader is familiar with. This technique is a way that authors can include history or literary tradition without explanation because the reader is assumed to share it with the author. Angelou makes use of allusion a great deal; for example when some poor white girls mock Momma in chapter 5, Maya launches into "Bread of Heaven," or when at her middle school graduation, the students, parents, and teachers sing "Lift Ev'ry Voice and Sing." Even the aphorisms her mother and grandmother readily dispense assume the reader understands the long tradition from which such sayings come.

Angelou's use of allusion is perhaps one of the strongest features of her writing. It allows her to take the work of other writers (like Paul Laurence Dunbar and Frances Ellen Harper), with whom the black community is familiar but who may be little known to white popular culture and make them accessible.

# 4 "Bringing the Gifts that My Ancestors Gave"—Angelou's Poetry

There is no doubt Maya Angelou was one of the most prolific writers of our time. In this chapter, we will look beyond the autobiographies to her poetry, books for children, and some of the pieces she wrote for popular magazines. We begin the chapter with an examination of two of Angelou's poems: "Hopscotch," from her first collection, and "On the Pulse of Morning," the epideictic poem she wrote and delivered at the inauguration of President Bill Clinton.

Angelou published her first volume of poetry, *Just Give me a Cool Drink of Water 'Fore I Diiie,* in 1971. It was a bestseller and received a Pulitzer Prize nomination, although "critical reception was mixed."[1] Angelou had released the poems in the collection as recordings first, emphasizing their sound and rhythm, their "orality rather than traditional literary poetry."[2] Criticism seemed polarized: some was dismissive, such as that of John Avant, who claimed the work was "rather well-done schlock, not to be confused with poetry for people who read poetry."[3] Other reviews were filled with praise: "Angelou's poetry is economical, rhythmic, musical and confident."[4] Biographer Jacqueline Thursby writes that Angelou's poetry is accessible to everyone; that it "contributes to

**epideictic**

The language of formal events, most often a funeral.

In 1970 Maya Angelou's first volume of poetry was published.

building a community of understanding and meaning without being preachy or didactic."[5] She goes on to note that Angelou uses a wide range of poetic devices "that span language from beautiful and sublime to vulgar and even scatological because that is how real life is."[6]

## "Hopscotch"

One of Angelou's first collections is entitled *Just Give me a Cool Drink of Water 'Fore I Diiie* . The work is divided into two parts. The first contains twenty poems that describe "the whole gamut of love from the first moment of passionate discovery to the first suspicion of painful loss."[7] In the second section of the book, Angelou turns her focus to "protest and anger at the situation of black America."[8] According to writer Sarah Johnson, these poems are generally judged to be the most successful in the collection.[9]

> Let's examine a poem from part two of the collection called *Harlem Hopscotch.*
>
> *One foot down, then hop! It's hot.*
> *Good things for the ones that's got.*
> *Another jump, now to the left*
> *Everybody for hisself.*
>
> *In the air, now both feet down.*
> *Since you black, don't stick around.*
> *Food is gone, the rent is due*
> *Curse and cry and then jump two.*
>
> *All the people out of work,*
>
> *Hold for three, then twist and jerk.*
> *Cross the line, they count you out.*
> *That's what hopping's all about.*

*Both feet flat, the game is done.*
*They think I lost. I think I won.*

In general, this poem has a rhythm like the sound of feet playing hopscotch: A player hops, is suspended in the air for moment, and then lands on a square. The beat is also reminiscent of bebop music.

In the first four lines of the poem, the narrator lets us know that we're going to be getting instructions ("One foot down, then hop!") It's also hot, but we already know that this game (called hopscotch) is really a metaphor for something else; so, too, is the heat. Hopping on one foot, the narrator jumps us into the concept that wealth follows wealth; even a child knows this. Furthermore, there's no altruism or charity here; everyone is looking out for him or herself.

**rhythm**

The recurrence of syllables at regular or expected intervals.

In the next two lines, the narrator tells us that if you're black, the only option is to keep moving. You can curse and cry all you want, but with no money or shelter you have no security. Moreover, you have no power. "To live in a world measured by such blunt announcements as 'food is gone' and 'the rent is due,' people need to be extremely energetic and resilient."[10]

The narrator next advises all the people who can't find work to wait, because really that is the only choice they have. There is pain in this position ("Hold for three, then twist and jerk"), but complaining, or "crossing the line" will only bring trouble ("they count you out"). Compounding the pressures of hunger, poverty, and unemployment is the racial bigotry that consistently discriminates against people of color. Life

**couplet**

Two successive lines of verse forming a unit that usually rhymes.

itself has become a brutal game of hopscotch.

And yet, in the couplet that finishes the poem ("Both feet flat, the game is done/They think I lost. I think I won."), the narrator tells us that winning and losing are all in the eye of the beholder. Though there may be nothing to show for all that hopping, the winner is the person who did not give up or conform to negative stereotypes.

### "On the Pulse of Morning"

In 1993, President Bill Clinton decided to invite a poet to read at his inauguration ceremony. It had been thirty-two years

## POETRY AS A VOICE

As an art form, poetry is sometimes ridiculed. Commentator Mary Schmich of the *Chicago Tribune* once wrote, "In many circles, poetry is known as the puffery of professors, the free-verse scrawl of lovelorn teens, rhyming whines to be shared, at best at the poetry slam at the local bar."[11] But for many, poetry does have it uses. A recent article in the London *Sunday Times* observed that during times of times of stress, people turn to poetry. For example, when Michael Brown was shot and killed in Ferguson, Missouri, a poem called "Good Bones" by Maggie Smith went viral on the internet.

On the other hand, poetry can serve as "the very language of defiance."[12] Angelou's poem "Still I Rise," has received much attention recently, with tennis star Serena Williams and pop singer Nicki Minaj both reciting it as a show of strength and resistance to prejudice.

since a poet had shared the stage with an incoming president (the last time had been 1961 when John F. Kennedy had invited Robert Frost). The poet President Clinton asked was Maya Angelou, and the piece she composed for the event, "On the Pulse of Morning," was so popular that after it was televised, it was published and distributed to schools, libraries, and bookstores across the nation. It earned Angelou the designation "people's poet."

Angelou greets Bill Clinton on stage at his 1993 inauguration.

"On the Pulse of Morning" is an optimistic poem, inviting all races, cultures, and religions to come together and examine what makes the nation great—in the past, the present, and the future.

> In the breadth of 106 lines grouped in 12 irregular stanzas, the poet Angelou admonishes injustices of the past, proffers recovery of the spirit, and stimulates hope for change. Specifically, her purpose is to convince the audience that traditions which have enslaved them can be challenged; that the darkness need not continue if the American people will look toward change, turn to each other with hope, and begin a dialogue.[13]

The poem opens with a Rock, a River, and a Tree in no specific location. Written in capital letters, it is as if these natural elements are more than just pieces of a landscape—they are distinct entities, each with their own magnificence, rather like the Holy Trinity. Angelou goes on to tell us that each of these have been "host to species long since departed." She mentions mastodons and dinosaurs, animals who are now extinct but who are still significant in that they left "dried tokens" and history of the past that we in the present can interpret. One interpretation of the poems suggests that reading aloud lines seven through eight reveals the rich sounds Angelou has crafted into the poem. "The repetition of long vowel sounds and the internal rhyme of 'Doom/is lost in the gloom' perhaps reflects the somber mood Angelou is setting while describing these extinct creatures."[14]

Beginning with the next stanza, Angelou moves us into the present tense, giving the Rock the ability to "cry out" to us. The Rock tells us that we can step on it to get a better vantage point and perhaps see our future, but warns us not to use it as a way of hiding from what might be unpleasant: "But seek no haven in my shadow."

In stanza three the poet speaks to us directly, informing us that we are "created only a little lower than/the angels," suggesting that humans are something divine and have more in common with the earth and the heavens than not. The Rock, who has seen dinosaurs and other species come and go, is turning its attention to humans who have been hiding in a "bruising darkness/Face down in ignorance." Angelou's choice of "bruising" is interesting. It conjures the image of a black and blue mark that might be the result of a rock that is thrown or might just be the shadow cast by the stone.

Angelou writes, "Your mouths spilling words/Armed for slaughter." One critic posits that she may have broken the line here to cause the reader to pause for a moment and consider what kind of words are coming out of human mouths. In fact, the words are harsh, flung out with little control.[15] Again the wise Rock admonishes the reader to stand on it and not hide.

In the next section of the poem Angelou introduces the River, singing "a beautiful song." The River invites the reader to come closer and sit beside it, while acknowledging that to get there the reader must travel "Across the wall of the world." This may be literal; that is, "some real geographic feature, or just representative of a boundary or obstacle on humankind's journey."[16]

The River compares each citizen of the United States to "a bordered country" and proceeds to describe how each of us has played a part in the negative actions of the nation such as war ("armed struggles for profit") and pollution ("collars of waste/My shore, currents of debris upon my breast"). It admonishes everyone and then informs everyone there is a place beside its banks only if we will "study war no more."

To the people who "Come,/Clad in peace," the River can offer its sage-like songs, passed down from "the Creator" who gave them at the dawn of time when the River and "the Tree and the rock were one." It was also the time "Before cynicism was a bloody sear across [the human] brow," that is, before selfish motivations marked humanity. By using the phrase "bloody sear," Angelou invokes the Bible, and the mark that Cain was forced to wear for murdering his brother.

Angelou starts the next stanza with a litany of nationalities and identities: Asian, Hispanic, Jew, African, Native American, Catholic, Rabbi, Priest, gay, straight, privileged, homeless, and so on, who hear the wisdom of a new element: the Tree. Like the River, the Tree encourages humanity to come and sit beside it and the River. For some this image conjures the inscription at the base of the Statute of Liberty ("Give me your tired, your poor, your huddled masses yearning to be free")[17] and therefore the great promise of the nation. The Tree also symbolizes stability—its roots tunnel deep into the earth—and as with a "family" tree, in this Tree every human has his or her place on its branches.

**litany**

A kind of prayer consisting of a long sequence of chanted appeals.

In line fifty-four, Angelou's River speaks again, defining the audience as American, a "descendant of some passed," and points out that before Europeans ever came to this country, it was the indigenous people (Pawnee, Apache, Seneca, Cherokee) who rested by its banks and devised names for all things. Yet, they were "Forced on bloody feet/Left me to the employment of/Other seekers—desperate for gain;" in other words, enslaved by those who came and exploited them and this land.

Lines sixty-three and sixty-four mention other cultures: Arab, Eskimo, Yoruba—another list that keeps the rhythm of the poem and underscores a coming together, a sharing of company. The first names in the list (Turks, Arabs, Swedes, Scots) represent those who came to this country willingly, the later names (Ashanti, Yoruba, Kru), came as slaves, "bought/Sold, stolen, arriving on the nightmare/Praying for a dream."

Continuing, the narrator now becomes the Tree, the Rock and the River, a composite of the natural world that belongs to all humanity, and all humanity's "passages have been paid." Regardless of what cultural history one comes with, the narrator admonishes us to "Lift up your faces" and consider "this bright morning dawning for you." Angelou continues "History despite its wrenching pain/Cannot be unlived, but if faced/With courage, need not be lived again." In other words, we will move forward by learning from the pain of injustice, not by redressing past wrongs. This repeats the sentiments in lines eleven and twelve, when the Rock told us to "seek no haven in my shadow," Angelou ends the stanza with short, tight lines, "perhaps wishing to slow the pace before the complete stop of the section break."[18] Images of daybreak, birth, and light underscore the bright, hopeful tone of the poem.

The next stanza begins with a call to everyone—woman, children, and men—to take their most private thoughts and mold them into something public. Though Angelou does not spell out what these private thoughts might be, many critics suggest that what Angelou is referring to is the basic needs of all humans—life, freedom, security—"In this sense these lines are a call to action, an encouragement to emphasize the importance of human rights."[19] Angelou now asks that we lift our hearts—the very essence of what makes us alive. She tells us, "Each new hour holds new chances/For a new beginning," that we should cast away our fears and give up the yoke of "brutishness."

As the poem nears its end, Angelou returns us to the Rock, the River, and the Tree; in short, to the rocks, rivers, and trees that make up the entire country. Now our attention is drawn toward the future, "The horizon leans forward/Offering [us] space to place new steps of change." Angelou refers to Midas, the mythical king who turned everything to gold with his touch, standing next to "the mendicant," a beggar, as if to say that the very privileged have a place next to those less fortunate on the "pulse of this fine day." There is a sense of hope and rebirth here, as Angelou seems to be confirming that this is a new dawn for humanity. She ends the poem with a simple request: look out at your fellow humans and say good

## Controversy

In April 2015, the *Washington Post* reported that the text on the Maya Angelou Forever Stamp uses a quote that Angelou did not actually write. The text on the stamp reads: "A bird doesn't sing because it has an answer, it sings because it has a song." When unveiling the new stamp, the US Postal Service incorrectly attributed the quote to Angelou and erroneously drew the connection to her autobiography *I Know Why the Caged Bird Sings*.

The postal service was not the only one to make the mistake: President Obama attributed it to Angelou in a presentation of the 2013 National Medal of Arts and National Humanities Medal. In numerous interviews, Angelou used the quote never attributing it to its true author. The line is actually from children's writer Joan Anglund Walsh and appears in her 1967 book of poems called *A Cup of Sun*.

Angelou in 2011, the year she published her last volume of poetry.

morning. Writes Linda Weldon-Martin, "The poem succeeds in creating what Jasmin DeGout terms 'a community of healing,' perhaps more so than had her shorter poems in the earlier collections."[20] Journalist Tavis Smiley calls the work, "a poem whose grand theme of radical inclusion conveyed a spirit of optimism with ringing clarity."[21]

### Critical Response to the Poem

Much has been made of the fact that Angelou was the first woman of color to recite poetry at a presidential inauguration. Most commentators agreed that her delivery was what made the moment especially weighty. "Eloquent and passionate" and "beautiful" were the words David Streitfeld of the *Washington Post* quoted several fellow poets as using.[22] But there were others who were less enthusiastic, among them poets David Lehman and Ishmael Reed, who thought that the work "seemed to meander a lot,"[23] and a staff writer at the *Economist* suggested that the poem "sounded like a mishmash of T.S. Eliot's 'Ash Wednesday' and 'The Politically Correct Handbook.'"[24]

Ultimately, the poem put Angelou's name in front of the public, prompting the *New York Times* obituary writer Margalit Fox to observe: "Though her memoirs, which eventually filled six volumes, garnered more critical praise than her poetry did, Ms. Angelou...very likely received her widest exposure on a chilly January day in 1993, when she delivered her inaugural poem, 'On the Pulse of Morning,' at the swearing-in of Bill Clinton, the nation's 42nd president."[25]

# 5 Other Writing

In addition to poetry, Angelou authored several cookbooks, containing not just recipes, but vignettes about them and her reflections on life, as well. In the view of many critics, these works were an extension of her serial autobiography. Some accused her of playing into the Aunt Jemima stereotype; in other words, the image of the African American slave who was the family cook, complete with a head wrap and mindless grin. But according to Professor Natasha Cole-Leonard, Angelou takes the image and turns it on its head with the recipes she offers up in her cookbook *Hallelujah! The Welcome Table*:

> Not only do we have the requisite collard greens, fried chicken, buttermilk biscuit, potato salad and pudding, but rarer delights such as pickled peaches, cackling corn bread and spoonbread...Such anticipated fare constitutes a full third of the text. But conscious of the limited perceptions that the public already holds of African American women as culinary artists, Angelou sets out to broaden their expectations.[1]

Angelou does this particularly well in a section entitled "Recipes from Another Country," which showcases recipes that her grandmother got from the women's page of a periodical the white women in Stamps used to get. "[H]er grandmother would entice one of the town's back domestic workers to smuggle her a used copy from the home of a white employer."[2] First her grandmother would critique the dishes, remarking

**vignette**

A brief story or scene.

over the stupidity of some of them, then she would ask Angelou to copy them out for her so she could experiment later. According to Cole-Leonard, that shows a certain kind of resourcefulness, an "act of subversion demonstrating a desire to fully experience the dominant culture and a refusal to be marginalized by Jim Crow domesticity."[3] In other words, both Angelou and her grandmother had gumption.

## Film and Television

In 1972, Angelou wrote the screenplay for a movie called *Georgia, Georgia*, and in so doing became the first African

Angelou played Nyo Boto, one of the main characters in the TV miniseries *Roots*.

American woman to write for film. The movie centers on Georgia, a black American singer who has made it big in Europe. She is touring in Sweden when she meets and falls in love with a white ex-patriot. Georgia's black maid and companion, Alberta, finds the relationship scandalous. As far as she is concerned, whites are no good, and her hatred fuels a rather explosive ending.

It's important to remember that 1972 was just eight years after the Civil Rights Act was signed into law. Many people (white and black) thought that races should not mix and were woefully uninformed. So Angelou taking on the topic was important. However, one critic felt that "unfortunately, Miss Angelou doesn't quite accomplish her goal in *Georgia, Georgia*. Though I found what I saw interesting and provocative, I left the theater feeling that several important questions about her characters were still unanswered."[4] Another critic echoes the sentiment that the themes are very wide-ranging:

> Maya Angelou's debut screenplay is nothing if not ambitious. She explores the loneliness of a single, successful woman at the top; the effect of the Vietnam experience on its shell-shocked vets and the plight of deserters who are permanently separated from their homes and families; the sicknesses of racism and obsession with racial purity; and the often poor choices that larger than life stars make for their inner circle (i.e. Elvis, Selena, Michael). Stockholm is just about the last setting you would expect for a penetrating drama on racial issues, and the setting is just one of several curveballs Angelou has in store.[5]

The film made a brief appearance in the United States and then fell into obscurity.

Angelou and rapper Common attend a benefit in 2008. The poet befriended many up-and-coming black artists.

Angelou made numerous appearances on television, from anchoring PBS specials to acting in the first version of Alex Haley's *Roots. I Know Why the Caged Bird Sings* was made into a TV movie in 1979 starring Diahann Carroll, Ruby Dee, Esther Rolle, Roger E. Mosely, Paul Benjamin, and Constance Good.

In 1993, Angelou made a small appearance in a film by John Singleton called *Poetic Justice.* The film centers around Justice (played by Janet Jackson), a young hairdresser who lives and works in South Central Los Angeles and who has just lost her boyfriend to a drive-by shooting. To deal with her grief, Justice writes poetry. Hired to work at a hair stylist's event in Oakland, Justice is stranded when her car breaks down. But then she remembers that her friend Ieasha was going to hop a ride down to Oakland with her boyfriend Chicago, a postal worker who is heading there with a truck full of mail. Justice hitches a ride only to discover that Chicago's driving partner is Lucky (played by rapper Tupac Shakur), the postman who delivers mail to her shop and keeps asking her out. While Ieasha and Chicago deal with their own relationship problems, Justice must decide if she is ready to let someone into her life—and if Lucky is that man.

Singleton asked Angelou to write poems for Justice's character. According to one film critic, "The maturity and reflection of the poems ring false in the mouth of a character barely out of her teens. They also weigh heavily on the inexperienced Jackson. She is more comfortable and appealing telling Iesha that she's going on a diet because 'my ass is getting too big' than waxing poetic about 'The ride of my breasts/The grace of my style.'"[6]

According to Angelou, she had words with the film's star, Tupac Shakur. He was swearing and fighting with someone on

*Down in the Delta* was Angelou's debut as a movie director.

the set, so she pulled him aside and asked, "When was the last time anyone told you how important you are? Did you know our people stood on auction blocks, bought and sold so that you could stay alive today?"[7] Her words brought the rapper to tears.

In 1998, Angelou debuted as the director of a film called *Down in the Delta.* It is the story of a young urban mother, Loretta Sinclair, who neglects her children. Seeing the damage, Loretta's mother sends her daughter and grandchildren down to Mississippi, where Loretta's uncle runs a diner. Even though he has his own troubles (an aging wife with Alzheimer's), he takes in the trio. The inevitable culture clash ensues, but all emerge the better for it. Reviews were mixed, such as the one that appeared in the *St. Petersburg Times*: "This is definitely an actor's piece, guided by a director with literary sensibilities that allow scenes to breathe and expand with emotional detail."[8] However, the same reviewer writes that "Angelou and Goble [the screenwriter] may have stretched their small movie too far with so many topics of importance—crime, estrangement, financial pride and guilt, even a late detour into slavery—leaving *Down in the Delta* equally cluttered and touching."[9]

# 6

# Maya Angelou: Present Tense

Maya Angelou was an enormously public figure. Even after her death, she continues to be quoted and serves as an inspiration to people around the world. Her family has created and maintains a Twitter feed and Facebook page for her. She is the inspiration behind the See Forever Foundation and the Maya Angelou Schools program. The musician Prince once lent Angelou, who had an aversion to flying, his tour bus. Her friendship with Oprah Winfrey was legendary. As one

Angelou and Oprah Winfrey were lifelong friends.

Winfrey biographer noted, reading Angelou's writing was "a revelation to young Oprah. Later on, she and Ms. Angelou would become so close that the latter today tends to refer to Oprah as her spiritual daughter."[1]

In 2013, Singer Beyoncé launched a fragrance called Rise. According to an article in *Women's Wear Daily*, the perfume promoted "female empowerment" and was "influenced by a poem [presumably "Still I Rise"] by one of Knowles's favorite poets, Maya Angelou."[2] Beyoncé also posted birthday and death notices for Angelou on her website.

Often quoted in popular magazines such as *Red Book*, *Ladies Home Journal*, and *Ebony*, Angelou weighed in on topics from parenting to the African American diaspora (the movement of people from their established homeland). For African Americans, this movement began when their enslaved ancestors were first brought to the New World's shores. In more recent times (1920–1970), rural southern blacks found themselves moving in large numbers to northern states where opportunities for work and freedom from discrimination were supposed to be more plentiful. In a 2010 interview with *Redbook* magazine, she gave culinary advice, listing the ingredients essential to her cooking (Meyer lemon juice, onions, garlic, and celery, canned beans and curry and cumin powder) and her favorite comfort foods: greens, cornbread, and fried chicken.[3]

In 2009, Angelou made a cameo appearance in a film written and directed by comedian Chris Rock, called *Good Hair*. The film explores the industry of "black" hair, focusing in particular on the process of using chemical treatments to straighten, or "relax," the hair. The process sounds anything but relaxing. "It is a long, tricky and expensive business whose purpose is to get black women's hair to resemble European hair—the idea is to 'relax' the white people who come into contact with black women. Furthermore, black hair products are largely controlled and manufactured by white people. And yet Rock shows that black women have made this style their own—it is no cultural cringe to white people."[4] In the film, Angelou confesses that she got her first treatment at age seventy (though pictures of her taken before she was seventy indicate something different). About hair itself, she says: "I

Michelle Obama introduces Angelou at the Black Entertainment and Television (BET) Honors in 2012. Angelou was there to accept the Literary Arts Award.

would say that hair is a woman's glory and that you share that glory with your family," she told the comedian. "And they get to see you braiding it and they get to see you washing it. But it is not a bad thing or a good thing, it's hair."[5]

Angelou made dozens of talk-show appearances sitting alongside hosts such as Oprah Winfrey, Johnny Carson, Tavis Smiley, Larry King, and Arsenio Hall. Some of Angelou's last interviews were with Bob Schieffer on "Face the Nation," regarding the death of Nelson Mandela, the Association for Supervision and Curriculum Development (ASCD) on how to instill resilience in children, and of course, with Oprah Winfrey. Winfrey told an *Entertainment Tonight* reporter that she spoke with Angelou a few days before her death. "She was so proud that I was doing this movie [*Selma*], and she said, 'Take it, baby. Take it all the way,' because she was a part of the [civil rights] movement."[6]

Angelou was parodied, perhaps most notably by comedian David Alan Grier, who in the 1990s impersonated her as a spokesperson for products like Fruit Loops and Butterfingers. In 2008, Grier also did a spoof of her poem "On the Pulse of Morning." Writes poet Jason Schneiderman, "When I think of Maya Angelou, I actually think of David Alan Grier doing Maya Angelou on *Saturday Night Live* ('Don't lay a finger on myyyyyyyyy but-tah-finger')."[7] Schneiderman goes on to say that what he remembers most about Angelou is her "persona." Angelou's legacy may, in fact, be that persona. As one journalist stated: "People just want to be near Maya Angelou. She's not the grandest poet in the world—much of her verse these days winds up on Hallmark greeting cards…Though she bursts into song now and then, she's no polished chanteuse. And she describes herself as an 'adequate' actress. But 74 years into her life, there is something about Maya."[8]

# CHRONOLOGY

**1928–** Marguerite Johnson is born on April 4.

**1931–** Along with her brother, Bailey, she is sent to live with her maternal grandmother in Stamps, Arkansas.

**1935–** Bailey Sr. takes the children to St. Louis to live with their mother.

**1936–** Angelou is raped by her mother's boyfriend and stops speaking. The children return to Stamps.

**1937–1940–** Angelou begins speaking again; graduates from middle school in Stamps.

**1941–** Angelou and Bailey move to San Francisco.

**1944–** Drops out of high school and becomes the first black female cable car conductor in San Francisco.

**1945–** Returns to high school and graduates; gives birth to son Guy Johnson.

**1946–1951–** Works different jobs including "shake" dancer in a nightclub and short-order cook; enrolls in night school; meets Tosh Angelos, a Greek American sailor, and is married.

**1952–1954–** Ends marriage with Angelos; becomes a nightclub entertainer at San Francisco's Purple Onion; travels to Chicago and New York; joins the Harlem Writers' Guild and begins to study writing in earnest.

**1954–1955–** Tours twenty-two countries with the US State Department's production of *Porgy and Bess*.

**1957–1958–** Leaves the production to be with her son; sings in nightclubs in California and Hawaii; returns to New York where she continues theater work and appears off-Broadway in *Calypso Heat Wave*.

**1959–1960–** Meets Martin Luther King Jr. and joins the Southern Christian Leadership Conference to work for civil rights; writes, co-produces, and performs in *Cabaret* *for Freedom*; appears in *The Blacks*, written by French playwright Jean Genet.

**1960–1961–** Becomes involved with South African freedom fighter Vusumzi Make; relocates to be with Make in Cairo, Egypt; works as editor at the *Arab Observer*.

**1962–** Moves to Ghana where her son is seriously injured in a car accident.

**1963–1964–** Works as assistant administrator at the School of Music and Drama at the University of Ghana; is freelance writer to the *Ghanaian Times*.

**1964–1965–** Works as a features editor for the *African Review* in Accra; returns to the United States in 1965.

**1966–** Has a role in the play *Medea*; writes for a series of ten one-hour programs called *Black, Blues, Black*.

**1968–** *Black, Blues Black* is broadcast.

**1970–** *I Know Why the Caged Bird Sings* is published and nominated for the National Book Award; Angelou receives a fellowship from Yale University and works as writer in residence at the University of Kansas.

**1971–** Publishes volume of poetry entitled *Just Give Me a Cool Drink of Water 'Fore I Diiie*.

**1972–** Writes a full-length screenplay and score (*Georgia, Georgia*) that is later made into a film; the script is nominated for a Pulitzer Prize.

**1973–** Performs on Broadway as Mary Todd Lincoln's dressmaker in *Look Away*; receives a Tony Award; marries Paul de Feu.

**1974–** Publishes second autobiographical work, *Gather Together in My Name;* works as visiting professor at Wake Forest, Wichita State, and California State universities.

**1975–** Is appointed by President Ford to the American Revolution Bicentennial Advisory Council; receives a Rockefeller Foundation scholarship; publishes a second poetry collection, *Oh Pray My Wings Are Gonna Fit Me Well.*

**1976–** Publishes her third volume, *Singin' and Swingin' and Gettin' Merry Like Christmas*; named Woman of the Year in Communications by *Ladies Home Journal.*

**1977–** Stars in television adaptation of Alex Haley's *Roots.*

**1978–** Publishes the poetry collection *And I Still Rise* and a book-length poem called *Phenomenal Woman.*

**1979–** Writes television screenplay called *The Sisters.*

**1980–1981–** Divorces Paul de Feu; publishes *The Heart of a Woman* and accepts tenure as the Z. Smith Reynolds Professor of American Studies at Wake Forest.

**1983–** Publishes *Shaker, Why Don't you Sing*? (poetry collection) and writes the play *On a Southern Journey.*

**1986–** Publishes *All God's Children Need Traveling Shoes* and *Poems: Maya Angelou.*

**1987–** Publishes *Now Sheba Sings the Song*, a book-length poem.

**1989–** A collection of interviews called *Conversations with Maya Angelou* is published.

**1990–** Publishes poetry collection, *I Shall Not be Moved.*

**1996–** Directs her first film, *Down in the Delta.*

**2002–** Publishes *A Song Flung Up to Heaven.*

**2008–** Publishes *Letter to My Daughter*, dedicates it to "the daughter she never had but sees all around her."

**2010–** Publishes cookbook *Great Food, All Day Long: Cook Splendidly, Eat Smart.*

**2013–** Receives the Literarian Award, an honorary National Book Award for contributions to the literary community; publishes her final autobiography, *Mom & Me & Mom.*

**2014–** Dies at her home in North Carolina at the age of eighty-six.

# Chapter Notes

## Chapter 1. "Strong Black Birds of Promise"

1. Dolly M. McPherson, *Order Out of Chaos: The Autobiographical Works of Maya Angelou* (New York: Peter Lang, 1990), p. 5.
2. Jacqueline S. Thursby, *Critical Companion to Maya Angelou* (New York: Facts on File, 2011), p. 4.
3. Ryan Reed, "California," in *American History*, ABC-CLIO, 2000. Web.
4. Thursby, p. 4.
5. Ibid., p. 5.
6. Ibid.
7. Maya Angelou. *I Know Why the Caged Bird Sings* (New York: Ballantine, 2015), p. 16.
8. Ibid., p. 57.
9. Ibid., p. 61.
10. Ibid., p. 59.
11. Ibid., p. 67.
12. Ibid., p. 66.
13. Ibid., p. 87.
14. Ibid., p. 88
15. Ibid.
16. Ibid., p. 93
17. Ibid., p. 254.
18. Thursby, p. 6.
19. *I Know Why the Caged Bird Sings*, p. 278.
20. Ibid.
21. Maya Angelou, *Gather Together in my Name* (New York: Random House, 2009), Adobe Reader e-book, p. 14.
22. Ibid., p. 15.
23. Ibid., p. 81.

24. Ibid., p. 82.
25. Ibid., p. 112.
26. Ibid., p. 170.
27. John von Rhein, "'Porgy and Bess' a Milestone in America's Long Saga of Racial Politics," *Chicago Tribune*, November 16, 2008, http://articles.chicagotribune.com/2008-11-16/news/0811140287_1_porgy-and-bess-catfish-row-dubose-heyward.
28. Ibid.
29. Maya Angelou, *The Heart of a Woman* (New York: Random House, 1981), p. 107.
30. Ibid., p. 173.
31. Ibid., p. 174.
32. Ibid., p. 179.
33. Ibid., p. 191.
34. Ibid., p. 196.
35. Ibid., p. 267.
36. McPherson, p. 107.
37. *The Heart of Woman*, p. 257.
38. Maya Angelou, *All God's Children Need Traveling Shoes* (New York: Random House, 1986), p. 8. E-book.
39. Ibid., p. 52.
40. Ibid., p. 39.
41. Ibid.
42. Ibid.
43. Ibid., p. 115.
44. Ibid., p. 123.
45. Ibid., p. 124.
46. Ibid., p. 138.
47. Ibid.
48. Ibid., p. 142.
49. Ibid., p. 147.

50. Maya Angelou, *A Song Flung up to Heaven* (New York: Random House, 2002), p. 16.
51. Ibid., p. 57.
52. Ibid., pp. 64–65.
53. Ibid., p. 150.
54. Ibid.
55. Maya Angelou, *Even the Stars Look Lonesome* (New York: Random House, 1997), p. 70.
56. Maya Angleou, "Maya Angelou on Facing Evil," Transcript, November 15, 2016, http://billmoyers.com/episode/maya-angelou-on-facing-evil/.
57. Mary Jane Lupton, *Maya Angelou: A Critical Companion* (Westport, CT: Greenwood Press, 1998), p. 17.
58. Linda Wagner Martin, *Maya Angelou: Adventurous Spirit* (New York: Bloomsbury, 2016), p 157. E-book.
59. Thursby, p. 14
60. Gary Younge, "No Surrender," *Guardian*, May 24, 2002, https://www.theguardian.com/books/2002/may/25/biography.mayaangelou.
61. Billy Collins in Linton Weeks, "Hallmark of a Poet; at 74, Maya Angelou Greets a New Line of Verse and Many Old Fans," *Washington Post*, May 11, 2002, National Newspaper Premier. Web.
62. Ibid.
63. Bob Minzesheimer, "Angelou's Memoirs End with a 'Song;' Prolific, Private Author Moves on to Other Topics," April 2, 2002, *USA Today*.
64. "Maya's Poem in Praise of Hillary: Asked by the *Observer* for Her Thoughts, One of America's Most Admired Writers Urges People to Elect a Second President Clinton and 'Help Make This Country Wonderful,'" *Observer*, January 20, 2008.

65. Ibid.
66. Maya Angelou, *Letter to My Daughter* (New York: Random House, 2008), p. xi. E-book.
67. Wanda Coleman, "Coulda Shoulda Woulda: A Song Flung Up to Heaven," *Los Angeles Times*, April 14, 2002. Web.
68. John McWhorter, "A Song Flung Up to Heaven (Book Review)," *New Republic* 226, no. 19: 35-41. OmniFile Full Text Mega (H.W. Wilson), EBSCOhost. Web.
69. Maya Angelou, "At Long Last, Ready for the Real Deal," *Washington Post,* January 18, 2009.
70. F. R. Lee, "Schomburg Center in Harlem acquires Maya Angelou Archive," *New York Times*, October 27, 2010. Web.
71. Thursby, p. 16.

## Chapter 2. Defying Odds and Gods Angelou and Autobiography

1. Romita Choudhury, *Rewritten Afro-American Autobiography* (ProQuest Dissertations Publishing, 1991).
2. Ibid., p. 1
3. Dolly M. McPherson, *Order Out of Chaos: The Autobiographical Works of Maya Angelou* (New York: Peter Lang, 1990), p. 3.
4. Choudhury, p. 1.
5. Mary Jane Lupton, *Maya Angelou: A Critical Companion* (Westport, CT: Greenwood Press, 1998), p. 29.
6. McPherson, p. 4.
7. K. Kohlmeier, *The Serial Autobiographies of Mary McCarthy, Kate Millett, Julia Alvarez, and Jamaica Kincaid,* 2011, ProQuest Dissertations & Theses Global. (856901256), p. 1.

8. Maya Angelou in Jackie Kay, "The Maya Character," *Conversations with Maya Angelou* (Jackson: University Press of Mississippi, 1989), p. 195.
9. Lupton, pp. 34–35.
10. Linda Wagner Martin, *Maya Angelou: Adventurous Spirit* (New York: Bloomsbury, 2016), p. 5. E-book.
11. Barrett John Mandel, "The Autobiographer's Art," *Journal of Aesthetics and Art Criticism* 27, no. 2 (1968): 215–26.
12. George Plimpton, "Maya Angelou, The Art of Fiction, no. 119," *Paris Review*, http://www.theparisreview.org/interviews/2279/the-art-of-fiction-no-119-maya-angelou.
13. Maya Angelou in Lupton, p. 34.
14. David Levering Lewis, "A Transitional Time: *The Heart of a Woman*," in *Readings on Maya Angelou* (San Diego: Greenhaven Press, 1997), p. 133.
15. Lupton, p. 35.
16. Maya Angelou in Kay, p. 195.
17. Wagner, p. 114.

## Chapter 3. Caged Bird

1. Diane Telgen, ed. "I Know Why the Caged Bird Sings," *Novels for Students*, vol. 2. (Detroit: Gale, 1998), *Gale Virtual Reference Library*, p. 133. Web.
2. Elizabeth Alexander, "Dunbar lives!" *African American Review* 41, no. 2 (2007): 395, *Biography in Context*. Web.
3. Maya Angelou, *I Know Why the Caged Bird Sings*. (New York: Ballentine Books. 2009), p. 3.
4. Ibid., p. 21.
5. Ibid., pp. 14–15.
6. Ibid., p. 8.
7. Ibid., p. 7.
8. Ibid., p. 8.

9. Ibid., p. 54.
10. Ibid., p. 55.
11. Ibid., p. 60.
12. Ibid.
13. Ibid.
14. Ibid., p. 64.
15. Ibid., p. 70.
16. Ibid., p. 23.
17. Ibid., p. 79.
18. Ibid., p. 85.
19. Ibid., p. 86.
20. Ibid., p. 88.
21. Ibid., p. 89.
22. Ibid., p. 92.
23. Ibid., p. 93.
24. Ibid., p. 98.
25. Ibid., p. 101.
26. Ibid.
27. Ibid., p. 104.
28. Ibid., p. 110.
29. Ibid., p. 114.
30. Ibid., p. 118.
31. Ibid., p. 121
32. Harold Bloom, *Maya Angelou's* I Know Why the Caged Bird Sings (Broomall, PA: Chelsea House, 2004), p. 38.
33. Angelou, *I Know Why the Caged Bird Sings*, p. 132.
34. Ibid., p. 135.
35. Ibid., p. 136.
36. Ibid., p. 171.
37. Ibid., p. 173.
38. Ibid., p. 179.
39. Ibid., p. 183.

40. Ibid., p. 193.
41. Ibid., p. 195.
42. Ibid., p. 198.
43. Ibid.
44. Ibid., p. 202.
45. Ibid., p. 203.
46. Ibid., p. 209.
47. Ibid., p. 210.
48. Ibid.
49. Ibid., p. 211.
50. Ibid., p. 215.
51. Ibid., p. 38.
52. Ibid., p. 220.
53. Ibid., p. 226.
54. Ibid., p. 232.
55. Ibid., p. 213.
56. Ibid.
57. Ibid., p. 214.
58. Ibid., p. 242.
59. Ibid., p. 245.
60. Ibid.
61. Ibid., p. 249.
62. Ibid., p. 250.
63. Ibid., p. 251.
64. Ibid., p. 256.
65. Bloom, p. 49.
66. Ibid., p. 267.
67. Ibid., p. 268.
68. Ibid., p. 269.
69. Ibid., p. 270.
70. Ibid., p. 271.
71. Ibid.

72. Ibid., p. 272.
73. Ibid.
74. Ibid., p. 281.
75. Ibid., p. 282.
76. Ibid., p. 288.
77. Ibid., p. 289.
78. Sondra O'Neale, "On the Perception of Black Women," in Bloom, p. 62.
79. Ibid.
80. Telgen, p. 139.
81. Stephen Butterfield in Bloom, p. 56.
82. Ibid., pp. 56–57.

## Chapter 4. Bringing the Gifts that my Ancestors Gave

1. Sarah Johnson, "Maya Angelou," 2008, Literature Online Biography. Web.
2. Ibid.
3. John Avant quoted in Bloom, Harold, ed. *Bloom's Guide to Major Poets* (Broomall, PA.: Chelsea House Publishers, 2001), p. 19.
4. Mary E. Williams, ed. *Readings on Maya Angelou* (San Diego: Greenhaven Press, 1997), p. 136.
5. Jacqueline S. Thursby, *Critical Companion to Maya Angelou* (New York: Facts on File, 2011), p. 169.
6. Ibid.
7. Carol E. Neubauer, "Maya Angelou's Poetry Creates Hope," in Mary E. Williams, ed., *Readings on Maya Angelou* (San Diego: Greenhaven Press, 1997), pp. 136–137.
8. Johnson.
9. Ibid.
10. Neubauer, p. 138.

11. M. Schmich, "Maybe Poetry Has a Chance After All." *Chicago Tribune,* January 22, 1993 (1963-Current File). Web.
12. Bryan Appleyard, "But Still, Like Dust, I'll Rise" "You may trod me in the very dirt, Maya Angelou; We Turn to Poetry in Times of Need, but Can It Really Help? And Why Doesn't It Sell More Copies?" *Sunday Times* (London, England), July 24, 2016, 6. Academic OneFile. Web.
13. Donna M. Witmer, "Robert Frost and Maya Angelou: Poet-as-Rhetor in the Presidential Inauguration: Textual Symbols and the Symbol of Enactment," 1994, Masters theses. (2123). http://thekeep.eiu.edu/theses/2123, pp. 31–32.
14. "On the Pulse of Morning," in *Poetry for Students*, Marie Rose Napierkowski and Mary Ruby, eds., *Gale Virtual Reference Library* (Detroit: Gale, 1998), 3:276.Web.
15. Ibid.
16. Ibid., p. 277.
17. Ibid.
18. Ibid.
19. Ibid., p. 278.
20. Linda Wagner-Martin, *Maya Angelou: Adventurous Spirt* (New York: Bloomsbury Press, 2016), p. 160. E-book.
21. Tavis Smiley, *My Journey with Maya* (New York: Little, Brown, 2015), p. 19.
22. D. Streitfeld (1993, Jan 21). "The Power and the Puzzle of the Poem." *Washington Post*, January 21, 1993 (1974-Current File). Web.
23. Ibid.
24. "Verse and Worse," *Economist,* January 23, 1993, 326, 26. Web.

25. Margalit Fox, "Maya Angelou, Lyrical Witness to the Jim Crow South, Dies." *New York Times,* May 29, 2014. Web.

## Chapter 5. Other Writing

1. Natasha Cole-Leonard, "Maya Angelou's Hallelujah! The Welcome Table: a Lifetime of Memories with Recipes as evocative text; or, 'Ain't' Jemima's recipes," *Langston Hughes Review* (19:2) 2005, p. 67.
2. Ibid. p. 68.
3. Ibid. p. 93.
4. Peter Bailey in *New York Times Film Review* 1970-1972 (New York: New York Times, 1970), pp. 242–243.
5. Hal Horn, "Film Review: *Georgia, Georgia*," 1972, http://hornsection.blogspot.com/2009/08/film-review-georgia-georgia-1972.html.
6. Peter Travers, "Girlz n the Hood—*Poetic Justice* directed by John Singleton," *Rolling Stone*, August 19, 1993, 81. Web.
7. Maya Angelou, interview with George Stroumboulopoulo, 2013, https://www.youtube.com/watch?v=vVVA_siR-xg.
8. S. Persall, 1998, "Coming to Grips in the Delta Series: Movie Review," *St. Petersburg Times,* December 25, 1998. Web.
9. Ibid.

## Chapter 6. Maya Angelou: Present Tense

1. Marianne Ruuth, *Oprah Winfrey* (Los Angeles: Melrose Square, 1996), p. 64. E-book.
2. Peter Born, "Beyoncé's Expression Of Self," *WWD*, December 20, 2013, 8. Web.
3. Nicole Yorio, "Maya Angelou: What's Cooking in Poet Maya Angelou's Kitchen? Comfort Food for Body and Soul. Get a Big Helping of Her Wisdom Here (and Snag Seconds

from Her Cookbook, *Great Food, All Day Long*)," *Redbook*, December 2010, 194. Web.

4. Peter Bradshaw,"Film & Music: Film Reviews: Relax, Don't Do It: Clever and Funny, Chris Rock's Film About the Hairstyles of African-American Women Makes the Cut: *Good Hair*," *Guardian*, June 25, 2010. Web.
5. Maya Angelou, *Good Hair*, directed by Chris Rock (2009; Santa Monica, CA: Lionsgate, 2010), DVD.
6. Oprah Winfrey quoted in ETonline Staff, "Exclusive: Oprah on Her Last Conversation with Maya Angelou," May 30, 2014, http://www.etonline.com/news/146999_exclusive_oprah_breaks_news_on_maya_angelou_memorial/
7. Jason Schneiderman, "I Thought I Hated Inaugural Poems (But It Turns Out I Don't)," *American Poetry Review*, March–April 2012, 11+. Web.
8. "Hallmark of a Poet; At 74, Maya Angelou Greets a New Line of Verse and Many Old Fans," *Washington Post*, May 11, 2002. Web.

# Literary Terms

**aphorism** A short phrase expressing something wise.

**couplet** Two successive lines of verse forming a unit that usually rhymes.

**epideictic** The language of formal events, most often a funeral.

**first-person narration** A story that the author tells from his or her point of view.

**foreshadowing** A literary device used to suggest events that may be coming.

**litany** A kind of prayer consisting of a long sequence of chanted appeals.

**maxim** A known phrase that expresses a general truth about life or a rule about behavior.

**metaphor** A word or phrase comparing two objects to give clearer meaning to one of them.

**rhythm** The recurrence of syllables at regular or expected intervals.

**vignette** A brief story or scene.

# Major Works by Maya Angelou

## Autobiographies

*I Know Why the Caged Bird Sings*
*Gather Together in My Name*
*Singin'and Swingin' and Gettin' Merry like Christmas*
*The Heart of a Woman, Random House*
*All God's Children Need Traveling Shoes*
*A Song Flung Up to Heaven, Random House*
*Mom & Me & Mom*

## Poetry

*Just Give Me a Cool Drink of Water 'Fore I Diiie*
*Oh Pray My Wings Are Gonna Fit Me Well*
*And Still I Rise (new version published in 2001 as Still I Rise)*
*Shaker, Why Don't You Sing?*
*Poems, four volumes*
*Now Sheba Sings the Song*
*I Shall Not Be Moved*
*On the Pulse of Morning*
*The Complete Collected Poems of Maya Angelou*
*A Brave and Startling Truth*
*Phenomenal Woman: Four Poems Celebrating Women*
*Amazing Peace: A Celebration*
*Love's Exquisite Freedom*

## Essays

*Lessons in Living*
*Wouldn't Take Nothing for My Journey Now*
*Even the Stars Look Lonesome*

*Hallelujah! The Welcome Table*
*Mother: A Cradle to Hold Me*
*Letter to My Daughter*

## Children's Books

*Mrs. Flowers: A Moment of Friendship*
*Life Doesn't Frighten Me*
*(With others) Soul Looks Back in Wonder*
*My Painted House, My Friendly Chicken, and Me*
*Kofi and His Magic*
*Angelina of Italy*
*Izak of Lapland*
*Renie Marie of France*
*Mikale of Hawaii*
*Amazing Peace: A Christmas Poem*

# Further Reading

## Books

Labrecque, Ellen. *Who Was Maya Angelou?* New York: Grosset & Dunlap, 2016.

McPherson, Dolly. *Order Out of Chaos: The Autobiographical Works of Maya Angelou*. New York: Peter Lang Publishing, 1990.

Smiley, Tavis. *My Journey with Maya*. New York: Little, Brown, 2015.

Wagner-Martin, Linda. *Maya Angelou: Adventurous Spirt*. New York: Bloomsbury Press. 2016.

## Websites

**Academy of Achievement: Maya Angelou**
*www.achievement.org/achiever/Maya-Angelou*
Includes biography, photos, interviews, and an audio podcast.

**Maya Angelou: Official Site**
*www.mayaangelou.com/biography/*
Covers the author's life, works, and charities as well as latest news.

**Maya Angelou, Lyrical Witness of the Jim Crow South, Dies at 86**
*www.nytimes.com/2014/05/29/arts/maya-angelou-lyrical-witness-of-the-jim-crow-south-dies-at-86.html?_r=0*

**Obituary touches on Angelou's life and legacy.**
**Poetry Foundation: Maya Angelou**
*www.poetryfoundation.org/poems-and-poets/poets/detail/maya-angelou*
Discusses the author's work and influences; includes comprehensive list of writings.

# Index

## H



## I



## J



## K



## L



## M